Just Like That

....

Gina Thorne

Contents

Prologue

He is not a lover who does not love forever--Euripedes

Prologue:

The alarm wakes me out of a deep sleep. Hitting the snooze, I know I have ten minutes of snuggle time before my day begins.

I spoon into position as Patrick wraps his arms around me. Soft, warm kisses on the back of my neck send a warm tingle through my body. For the last few years, this is how we began our day. It is our way to connect before our busy lives separated us for a few hours. "It's time to wake up," he kisses my neck some more as his hand travels to my waist, whispering "I love you."

"I'm not ready," I say almost in a whine. "I need another hour or two, please."

"Not today, maybe on Saturday I can let you sleep in...come on rise and shine." He says this just as the alarm sounds again. I know it is finally time to get out of bed. Patrick rubs his hand under my rib, rolls me over, and then kisses me on the cheek before he heads to the shower.

I walk down the hallway. "Good morning, Sunshine," I say as I kiss my older son on the forehead to wake him up for school. Even though I know he is no longer a little boy, he hasn't begun complaining about momma kisses, yet. Well, except for in public. "Your dad is making you eggs and sausage. Hurry and get ready so you can have breakfast with him before he leaves for work." He stretches and moans. "Come on, get up. You have a big day ahead of you." Mason bend his back into another deep stretch rubs the sleep out of his eyes. His hair is getting a bit shaggy, but it suits him. He can let it grow as long I can still see his eyes ... that is our deal.

By the time my 13-year-old son is dressed, his dad has breakfast ready. I can hear the conversation from Peyton's room. "Are you excited about tryouts today?" Patrick asks, trying to help Mason focus on the day ahead. "When will the coach be making his decisions for the team?"

"Tryouts last a month, but the coach will start making cuts during the third week. We won't know the team until the last week. I'm only nervous about my new position. I have a good shot as mid-field, but I would like to try for keeper. The coach says he needs a tall, aggressive player in the goal. I can do tall, but I'm still working on aggressive," he jokes, knowing he still has a baby face and doesn't look very intimidating. At 5'10 Mason is one of the tallest players on the team. He is built like his dad tall and lean with well-defined muscles, a natural athlete.

I walk into the kitchen holding Peyton, who has rubbed his face on my shoulder trying to wake up. I watch my husband of 15 years talking sports with Mason. His face fully focused on his son. Mason looks like his father with his black Irish coloring with dark brown hair and green eyes, but his facial features are definitely from my side of the family. Mason's excitement shows in his eyes as he and his dad discuss the ins and outs of soccer. Patrick tells Mason that he will not be able to pick him up from tryouts because he has a full day of meetings ahead of him. He is planning on picking him up tomorrow.

I place my hand on Patrick's shoulder, and his hand comes up to cover mine. "Hey, little man," Patrick looks up a takes notice of Peyton. "Breakfast time." Like magic words, Peyton bolts out of my arms into Patrick's lap ready to eat. Peyton is full of giggles as he begins eating his breakfast. He tries to insert himself into the conversation with his brother and dad. Patrick smiles at me with a small chuckle and a look of pure bliss.

After a quick breakfast with his boys and kisses for me, Patrick leaves for the office. "Yes, daddy went bye-bye," Mason tells Peyton as walks him into my bedroom.

"Ready to get dressed?" I ask Peyton. "What are you going to wear today?"

"Red. I want red." He's a bit opinionated for an 18-month-old, and his dark brown eyes sparkle as he bounces out of my room to find a red shirt. Mason chases him down the hall to help with pants and shoes. I am so lucky. I know we have only been a family for a short time, but the boys have a very special bond. After the birth of Mason then two miscarriages, the idea of another child in my house seemed to be impossible. Adopting Peyton was one of the easiest decisions we have ever made. My irresponsible cousin Gina lost custody of Peyton even with a year of intervention by the state. Instead of letting him go live with strangers, Patrick and I petitioned the court to let us adopt. Gina signed over, or rights to us, and his adoption was finalized just as the school year began. I took off from work, teaching third grade, for five weeks for 'maternity' leave to bond with my new baby. He has brought so much more life and happiness to our house.

As we leave the house, Patrick calls to tell me he will be out of the office for most of the day. He might not be home until after 7:00, but he would call before he headed home. I like how he keeps me informed of his day so that I don't worry about him. "I love you, have a great day. Wish Mason luck for me," he tells me before he hangs up.

Before letting Mason out at school, I remind him that I have a faculty meeting and will be there to pick from soccer as soon as I the meeting is over. After dropping Mason off at junior high and Peyton at daycare, I head off to work.

Mason calls me at 4:30 as the faculty meeting wraps up. "Hey, son, what's wrong?" I ask, not expecting his phone call.

"What time are you going to be here? I'm the last one at practice, and my coach is wondering if I've been forgotten?" He snickers. "Really, we just finished. I was just hoping you were on your way."

"Don't try to scare your momma like that. I'll be there in five."

Mason helps me pick up Peyton from daycare. When Peyton sees his big brother still in his soccer gear, he runs at him doing a great impersonation of Andes Cantor's "Gooooooal!" Mason's fist bumps him, "Yeah, little dude."

"Ok, off to the grocery store, then dinner and homework," I say to Mason.

"What time will dad be home? I have algebra homework tonight. No offence mom...you can help me with history and English, but we both know dad is better at math." I make a face at him and pretend his words wounded me. Even though I took calculus in college, I don't remember much of my higher math. I guess it's true if you don't use it you lose it.

God gave me you for the ups and downs plays as I pull my phone out to answer. "Hey, babe," I say to Patrick.

"I just called to let you know my last meeting finished early. I should be home for dinner, no later than 6:00. Tell Mason, I'm looking forward to finding out about tryouts. Is there anything you need from me before I head home?"

"No, we just left the store. Peyton wanted noodles for dinner...so spaghetti it is. I'll see you in a little while."

"I love you."

"I love you, too," I say as I end the call.

It is 6:30 and dinner is ready, but Patrick is not home, yet. Mason had finished all of his homework except for algebra. He helps set the table and sits Peyton in the booster seat. Spaghetti is everywhere within two minutes, but Peyton is happy with his noodles that I don't worry about cleaning up, yet.

As soon as dinner is finished, I set off to give the little man a bath. The water is warm, and he immediately begins to splash when he gets in the tub. His eyelashes are wet, and he is giggling each time his small hand hits the water. "Big splash, do it again," he tells me as he plays in the water. I squirt the shampoo in my hands then lather his hair. "I do it," he announces and begins to rub his hair mimicking my motions. I fell in love with this little guy the minute I saw him when he had just turned one, and four months later and he was officially a Cahill.

It's just after 7:00. "I thought dad would be home by now," Mason says as he enters the bathroom. I reach down to pluck Peyton from the tub and wrap him in a large bath towel.

"Well, maybe he didn't finish as early as he thought he would. Do you want my help with algebra? I just need to read over your examples, and I should be able to help you understand," I tell him, hoping that he took good enough notes to trigger my memory.

I put Peyton in bed and proceed to help Mason with homework hoping that Patrick hurries home to rescue me. Making a quick phone call to check of Patrick, I'm sent straight to voicemail. I leave a message.

I send Mason to bed at 9:30 and still there is no Patrick. I make another phone call to find out what time he is going to be home, but again I'm sent straight to voicemail.

Just after 10:00 there is a knock on the door, and like that my world is turned upside down.

Chapter 1 - Moving

The future is completely open, we are writing it moment to moment
-- Pema Chodron

Chapter 1 - Moving

Emily's POV:

2 months later-

breath in - breathe out - breathe in - breathe out....

Looking in the mirror I ask myself, "Why is this so hard?" I think to myself, "Because you are packing up your whole entire life and heading back home with my tail tucked between my legs." This is not what I had planned. After fifteen years of marriage, I am a single mom with two children. This is not how I wanted for my life. This is not how I wanted to go back home. Patrick and I planned to move home for his last assignment, and stay after his military service was finished we even bought (built) a house in the same neighborhood as my older brother C.J., Christopher James Daniels, but now he will not be coming with us. I am trying not to be angry and bitter, but today that is going to be hard to do.

"Emily? You ready to go? The movers will be here any minute," I hear my mother say from my bedroom door. "Honey, it will be ok. I'm here, your dad is here, you have two wonderful sons, you can do this," I expel a big breath and pull my shoulders up and put on my game face, it's show time. No one needs to see how hard this is.

My dad just left with the boys. He was going to spend the day with them and check into our hotel suite while the house is being packed away. My parents flew in two days ago to help me move out of this house. They were not crazy about me being the only driver on what will be an almost 24 hour drive to my new house. I'm not going to lie I was not looking forward to doing this alone. I've found it difficult sometimes to be the only parent, but being an only parent and moving was more of a challenge than I was ready for.

My mom, Hannah Daniels, is wonderful. She is a few inches taller than my 5'4" body, but you would think she was six feet tall. She is very much the take charge kind of person. Watching her the past few days has given me strength to see this through. She is spending the day with me making sure all the items are packed correctly and labeled for the new house. I'm moving from a three bedroom ranch style house to a four bedroom two story house with a full walkout basement. My kids, well mostly Mason, are looking forward to the having a lot more space. Since we will be living in the same neighborhood as my older brother and his wife and their three kids and not too far from my younger brother Michael, Patrick and I had opted for a larger home so we could entertain family.

I smile at myself in the mirror, hoping that it will convince my mom that everything is was ok. "Alright, ready mom. Let's get this done," I reply as she lets the packers into the house.

She gives a quick smile and says, "You sound like your dad." Looking at her I can see myself in 25 years. We share the same large blue eyes (but mine are not as blue as they used to be) that do not disappear when we smile. Her dark hair is just now starting to turn gray and with her high cheek bones she doesn't come close to looking as old as her 62 years. Even though I have the lighter complexion and hair color of my dad, many of my features come from the lady that stands in front of me. I hope I age as well as she has.

I watch the packers as they carefully wrap and box everything I own. I help when I can, answer questions when they arise, and direct traffic through my house. Like some synchronized dance, the packers waltz through removing all evidence that Mason, Peyton, and even Patrick or I have ever lived in this home. In less than six hours the packers were finished and out of my house.

At the hotel I changed my clothes and grabbed my camera and made my way down to the pool, where I found my dad in the middle of splash fight with Peyton and dad against Mason. "You're here early. You joining us or are you hitting the hot tub?" he asks. Peyton splashed the water hard enough to reach Mason, and a fit of giggles erupts from his little mouth. I couldn't help laughing with him. Mason tried to look upset that Peyton was able to get him wet. Then, he exited the pool and cannon balled right near my dad, and he drenched both of them.

I pick up my camera and snap pictures of the men in my life, playing. Mason jumps on my dad's back and tries to dunk him and fails miserably. Peyton sits on the steps with his floaties cheering on his grandpa. Dad grabs my tall, lanky son with one hand and sweeps his feet out from under him and sends his flailing body deep in the pool. After a few more dunks, Mason quickly swims to Peyton in hopes that his little brother can save him from his grandpa. I smile and feel happy at the precious sight before me. My dad is having a great time, chasing the boys around the pool. My boys are lucky to have such an active and involved grandfather. They are going to need a good man to be an example for them. I am glad my father will be there for them. How did I think I could do all of this by myself?

I must have looked a little lost in my thoughts. Mason stares at me with a bit more concern than a teenage boy should have for his mom. His expessions look so much like his father's, and he is tall, dark and oh, so handsome. His green eyes sparkle as he tells me, "Mom, your turn, join us." Flashing a super fake, cheesy smile, "Oh, please. Oh, please, Oh, please! I'll be your favorite son, if you do." Laughing I agree that it's time to relinquish the camera to my mom and join my boys and dad in the water. Peyton is excited to swim with me for a while. We both enjoy the Mason/Papa show for a while with Peyton cheering for his brother this time. My mom encouraged the horseplay and snapped of all the excitement.

After an hour we exited the pool, cleaned up, and changed for dinner. "Ok, so what happens tomorrow?" my dad asks, knowing that he's with me and my mom will be keeping the boys occupied. He places a hand on my shoulder as we head out of the hotel to a nearby restaurant. My dad, James (Jim) Daniels, is just shy of six feet and at 5'4" I have to lean my head back in order to look at my dad's face. It won't be long until Mason is taller than him, and maybe he will be taller than Patrick by the time he quits growing. He'll be fourteen soon and he is only a couple of inches shorter than his papa, but he is still growing.

"The moving truck will show up at 7:30. They estimated the job will take about 5 hours to load and pull out. Hopefully, we can be on the road early enough to make it at least to New Mexico tonight. Our biggest job is to check off each item that is being loaded onto the truck, so we have it for our records." I smile at him to help him with the worried expression on his is showing me. He spends too much time worrying about me.

Over his shoulder I catch a glimpse of my two sons playing keep away with the salt shaker. Every time Peyton wins he twists his face into a baby smirk and yells, "Oh, yeah" mimicking what Mason does with his friends from the neighborhood. My boys are the light of my life. Even though Peyton is not my biological son, he and Mason do share some similarities. They both have dark brown hair, but Mason's will probably turn almost black like his father's. They also have the same sweet but mischievous sparkle in their eyes, and when they smile it is from ear to ear.

"You are a bit too much like your brother," I tell him. Peyton nods his head, and Mason shakes his head and adds a "you wish" in Peyton's direction. My boys are a great distraction in the midst of all of these changes.

After dinner we head off to bed to prepare for the long day ahead.

I wake up in a panic. The clock reads 3:25...breathe in, breath out, breathe in, breathe out. I walk to the bathroom to through some water on my face. "Don't cry, don't cry," I tell my reflection. It's just a dream, it can't hurt you. I am unable to go back to sleep, so I lay there until my alarm sounds at 6:30.

"Emily, honey, it's time to go," my dad says as he knocks on my door. "Hannah has the boys. Let's get this done."

Jim's POV:

I've watched my daughter all day as she checked each of the packed boxes and wrote the information on the clipboard. She's all business. She is beautiful and strong, but these past few months have changed her. No longer is she bubbly, lively and free spirited...she seems so lost and broken. No parent wants to see their child suffer, especially one as sweet and loving as my Emily. She is doing all she can and more to be strong for her boys, but she is still my little girl. I can't protect her from everything, but having her closer to me will make it easier for the whole family. I'm glad she agreed to go ahead a move back home. Without Patrick by her side, she is going to need all the love and support our large family can provide. With her brothers, aunts and uncles and a big slew of cousins...she will be taken care of and so will her boys.

Hannah and I have to get her out of this place. It holds too many memories and she is drowning...I can see it. She is too stubborn to tell anyone that she needs help, that is why I haven't given her a choice. Hannah and I flew across the country to help her, if she wanted us to or not. She looks tired. I heard her up early this morning.... did she even sleep last night? If I ask, will she tell me the truth? I doubt it. Knowing her she was up during the night worrying about things she cannot change. This is not her fault, but I know she probably blames herself.

"Emily," I say as I place my finger on her chin and lift her face to mine. "You're doing a great job with everything." She exhales deeply as she understands the full meaning of my words. I see her eyes fill with tears, but none fall. Oh, this is the first time she has shown me what she is feeling. I knew she was hurting, but she sure wasn't going to show that to me or her mom. I bet she doesn't let anyone know. I pull her into a big hug. She nuzzles into my chest and I feel her body relax in my arms. I hold her for a few minutes and kiss her gently on the top of the head. "I love you," is all we say.

"The truck is loaded. We need to get on the road if we're going to make it to the new house by Friday to meet truck." It was Tuesday, but we have two long days of driving and with a almost two year old we are going to have to make frequent stops.

"Yeah, dad, I'm ready. Let's go make some new memories."

"That's my girl." She looks up at me with a smile that doesn't even begin to reach her eyes. This is the same smile that she has given me and Hannah for the last few days. She looks hollow and a little bit lost. "I know this is not what you had planned, but you're not going home a failure. You are doing what is best for the boys and yourself. You all need this."

With a half smile, she agrees and opens the door to her Honda to go pick up Hannah and the boys, and get on the road. I pull out behind her in the suburban, loaded down with all of our luggage and baby gear

----

please vote

Check out the picture of Mason and the video from Mat Kearney posted with this chapter

Chapter 2 - All Roads Lead Home

W hen trouble comes, it's your family that supports you -- Guy Lafleur

Chapter 2 - All Roads Lead Home

Emily's POV:

"Just follow behind your dad. He's got the whole route planned out," Mom informs me. "We may only get about five hours in to the journey, but every mile is taking us home."

My mom smiles and continues, "I'm so glad you've decided to move back home...I've really missed you."

"I'm not really moving home."

"You know what mean. This is the first time since Mason was born that you have lived within a day's drive, let alone within a 2 hour drive." She was right. Home has been "where the military sends you." The closest that I have lived to my family has been almost 900 miles, when Patrick and I moved to South Carolina. We had gotten stationed there for a short time after he had made rank. Within two years we were moving again, as he took over command of a unit in North Carolina. We left North Carolina for New Mexico, then to southern California...now I'm moving without my husband, without the military...it's a bittersweet ending to a wonderful way of life.

Mom smiles at me; she's waiting for me to talk. She is trying to give me space, but I can see she wants me to share my feelings. She just wants to help...I am not ready, yet. Thankfully, she does not ask me questions, and she has not brought up the subject of Patrick. We fall into a comfortable discussion about our relatives. I got caught up on all the family gossip...who is married, engaged, divorced, pregnant, and/or any combination...this makes me wonder what my relatives say about me. I just don't want pity.

Mason's POV:

"How are you doing," Papa asked me just as we pulled out of the parking lot.

"I'm good. I'll miss this place, but it's not the same as it was...Actually, I'm looking forward to being closer to my cousins. Uncle C.J. told me we'll only be two blocks away from his house."

"That's good, but that's not what I mean. How are YOU doing?" He emphasized the word you, and immediately understood. He was asking about my dad. I am not going to lie.

"It hurts, but I'm working through it, but Mom..." My I didn't know how to tell Papa that I'm worried about my mom. She acts like nothing happened, like dad will magically come back into our lives and we will be a family again.

"Son, this isn't easy for anyone...especially not your mom. She is a very strong woman and she will be ok. She's got a lot of support waiting for her at home. Has your mom talked to you about your new school?" Yeah, change of subject. It's hard dealing with all the issues from my dad, and I do not want to talk about all that, yet.

"A little...I know the school has a soccer team and tryouts are at the end of January. It seems weird. At my old school we tried out in the fall and it took a month. He we tryout in the spring and it takes two weeks. What gives?"

"Well, soccer isn't that big a deal here. Football is king and basketball and baseball are princes...soccer is like the ugly step child." I snarl my nose at his comment. "That shouldn't stop you, son. You have a passion for the sport...that's what matters. What position are you trying out for?"

"I'd like to play keeper. That's what I was trying for when dad...." I couldn't finish my thought. "I'm going to let the coach know I can also play midfield. I just want to play soccer. I don't really care what position. It won't be the same without dad in the stands. If I make the team, will you come to one of my games?" I try to not sound so desperate, but I miss my dad. I wish he hadn't left us.

"You give me the schedule and I'll be at every game." That would be great. If I can't have dad, then I can have Papa there for me even if he doesn't know much about the sport.

I look back to see what Peyton is doing. He's been quiet for a while now, and he was sound asleep. He probably was tired or bored or both. My baby brother is a cool kid, but I'm glad he's asleep because I need a break.

"You're really a good big brother. You know he looks up to you, and without your father around he is going to mimic what you do. I know you're a great help to your mom, but make sure you show Peyton how your mom should be treated...how a lady should be treated. In saying that, don't forget you're a kid. BE a kid! You're not your dad, and you're not Peyton's dad...don't forget you are kid and a brother have fun." I know he doesn't mean KID in a bad way, but I like it when my mom calls me "young man."

"I won't, but I worry about her. I sometimes think she is trying to make up for dad. You know, she cried for a whole week, and then she stopped. She cried all the time for a week, and then one day she just quit. She's only cried once since then and not even in front of me...but I heard her."

"Give your mom some time...she will be fine. It may take a little while, but she'll be fine. Your uncles and I will be around...we help take care of her. You could do me a favor. You could talk to us when you have concerns, even what you think may be silly ones. That way, we will know how to help your mom."

"I think I can do that. The mood in here is thick. It's time for music appreciation." I laugh as my papa makes a face.

"The only appreciation will be you appreciating my music. You headed south, so country music it is." Now he laughs while I make a face.

"I don't want to hear any twangy mess."

Papa laughs some more. "Don't worry. I'll play something you might like." With that, Papa turned on the satellite radio to some country music station I've never heard of. The display showed -Josh Turner Will you Go With Me.

"Hey, Papa that's a mandolin. I keep asking mom for one of those. Mumford and Sons music has a mandolin...I like Little Lion man. I can play it on my guitar, but it doesn't sound the same.

"So, this is country music. It's not bad, but I don't think I would choose it for myself. "

My Papa smiled at me. "You've been playing guitar a long time. So you play anything else?" he asked me.

"I play rhythm, electric, and base guitar and sometimes the keyboard...that's it so far."

Papa and I had a nice talk until Peyton woke up needing a drink. So much for a long nap...I don't even think he slept an hour.

Emily's POV:

Peyton was a trouper for his Papa. We were hoping for five hours of driving before we were too tired to carry on. Mason kept Peyton busy with conversations about toys, singing songs and watching Pixar movies... it wasn't until we were almost to Flagstaff before Peyton finally faded for the second time.

"Tomorrow we'll be able to take in some sites as we travel. We're only five hours from Albuquerque. I think we should start early, and try to get there about noon. It would be nice to take the tram up to the top of the mountain for lunch. Peyton would love it, and you already know that Mason does," my dad says as he plans the rest of our trip. "Giving Peyton some time to run around will make the trip easier on all of us." I give him a sign a small smile that says thank you. "You're doing just fine," he says as I melt into his big arms.

"I know this is tough, but you have us and your brothers...you will NOT be alone raising these two boys."

Mom comes out to help us with the overnight bags. I take Peyton out of his car seat and get the room key from my mother. "Thanks Dad," I say as I head off to my hotel room with my sons.

The next morning at breakfast, Mason decided it was his turn to ride with me. I think it was because I would let him control the music. Peyton rode with his Mimi and Papa.

"Alright Mom, it's time for music appreciation," Mason says with a wide smile.

"Woah, wait a minute buster...this will not be a repeat of our last trip to LA. Music appreciation means you have to appreciate my music, too!" I thought Mason's eyes were going to roll out of his head.

"Of course, I wouldn't have it any other way," he was able to say with a limited amount of sarcasm.

"I'm very happy you did not choke on those words as they exited your mouth..."

"Ha, funny mom."

Mumford and Sons, Jack Johnson, Adele, and Arcade Fire kept us entertained as we drove to Albuquerque. My mom called us a few times to let us know they needed gas, or Peyton needed a break, or to find out what we were listening to...because we looked like we were having a whole lot of fun. We were.

After a short stop in New Mexico, we pressed ahead and made it to Amarillo just after dark. Mason could not wait to get out of the car and into the indoor pool at the hotel. Dad and Peyton were almost as excited, but not quite.

After two and a half days of driving we made it to mom and dad's house. We would have to leave fairly early to meet the moving truck at the new house. Now that I'm back in Arkansas, I am excited. This is my home, where I'm comfortable, and where my family is. Even though my parents moved away in favor of the river shortly after Patrick and I were transferred to South Carolina, this is home.

We have played musical cars for the last few days as we drove from southern California to my childhood home in Arkansas. Through the last leg of our journey, Peyton and Mom are with me...Dad and Mason are doing some "male bonding."

It is just over an hour drive from my parent's home at the lake to my new house. Turning into my new neighborhood, I take note of the different large houses, the gated areas, the golf course that sets prominently in the center, and the walking trail. Patrick and I had looked into this area before...I chose to build a modest home in this rather intimidating area. My new home is large for me but a bit small for the surrounding homes. It backs up to a nature reserve, and has a small path that leads to the walking trail. Even though it is in a very large neighborhood, it feels quite secluded.

As we turn down my street, there were an abundance of cars littering the side of my street. On further inspection, the owners of those cars seemed to be congregated on my front lawn. My brothers were standing front and center of the large group holding a sign that said, "Welcome Home Em, Mason and Peyton." There had to be at least 30 people there clapping and waving, greeting us as we moved back to Arkansas. My family is something else. I can't help but chuckle at the sight.

"Oh, my god, are you kidding me? Mom did you know about this?" I ask while I chuckle and shake my head.

"This is C.J.'s idea of a small gathering. You know your brother. He's a little bit excited to have is sister close."

I catch C.J's smug look as we watches me exit the car. He smiles at me and his hazel eyes have a bit of mischief in them just like always. I have missed the way he could always make me laugh. Even though he is built like a linebacker, he is nothing more than a big old teddy bear. He runs to me a gives me a hug, and I can't help but melt into my big brother's strong arms. His hugs always make me fill safe and protected.

"I can't believe you did this."

"What? It's not every day that my sister decides to move back home...near the greatest brother in the world."

"Are you talking about me?" Michael says laughing in my ear as he hugs me from the back. "Hey, it's an Emily sandwich." With that they proceeded to squeeze the air out of my lungs...seems like old times.

"Ok, ok, let me breathe." Oh, how I missed my brothers.

"I'm glad you're back," Michael says with a big smile, then proceeds to pick me up and take me to the crowd. Most of the crowd are relatives of one kind or another, but there are a few people from high school. Mason joins us with Peyton, and I set off introducing my sons. After 20 minutes of hellos and hugs the moving van showed up.

My sister-in-law Keira, C.J.'s wife, took Peyton and my youngest nephews with her. "Let me take Peyton so you can get your house in order. He will be fine with me and the boys. I'll be back with dinner at 6:00 let me know if you need me sooner," she said with a smile and a big hug. "I'm so glad you're back, so is C.J."

"Thanks, I appreciate your help and I'm glad I'm home, too." My thoughts drifted back to Patrick. Keira must have noticed.

"I'm here for you if and when you need me." She smiled and picked up Peyton.

"I wanna go to your house," he said with a large beaming smile. I kiss him goodbye and tell him to be a good boy for Aunt Keira. "I be good Momma," he replies and waves to me as he leaves.

My dad talks with the driver of the moving truck, while I go inside the house with Michael. He helps me decide where all of my furniture and things will go. He is always good at helping me make decisions. He gently guides me from one room to another. Michael had built this house for me and Patrick. It wasn't suppose to be finished for another month or two, but after what happened with Patrick, Michael put a rush on to get me back home sooner. It's a good thing. I will here for Christmas and New Year, and Mason can start school when it is back in session in January.

As my belonging began to exit the moving truck, I thought most of the crowd would leave. I was shocked as many of them staked out rooms in my house and began to help unpack and organize. Even though not everything was put away, by dinner time my kitchen was organized, all three bedrooms were unpacked and cleaned up, the guest room had a bed, and my living room was useable. Just before 6:00 Keira returned with 10 boxes of pizza for the crowd.

I took a deep breath and with a smile I looked at all the people that I loved.

Peyton was happy to see his big brother. "I wanna play wiff you," he told Mason. As Mason took off to the backyard with his brother, he came bolting right back into the house...very excited. "Mom, you gotta see this. Someone left a soccer goal in the backyard."

I stare at him. "Surely not." About that time my eyes found my brothers, they smirked at each other. "You guys are going to spoil my boys."

"You got it sis," Michael smiles at me.

"They're the only nephews I have- we need to spoil them," C.J. adds.

I give each of my brothers a kiss, "Thanks."

After we ate pizza, most of the crowd started to leave. Mom and Dad still had a bit of travel time to make it back to their home. My brothers and I sat in the living room, looking out at the back yard. Even though the nature preserve was technically not my property, it made my backyard feel like it went on forever.

"Hey sis, want a beer?" C.J. asked as he popped the top of his.

"Yea, how about a Boston Lager."

"Emily, come here." I walked over to Michael and looked out onto the backyard. "See that path? That will take you to the walking trail. I had the workers clean out the brush so you could have easy access."

"Thank you. That's wonderful. As soon as it gets a bit warmer, I plan to use the trail a lot."

C.J. came back with beer, and Mason pulled up a chair and joined us. "Peyton fell asleep watching Cars. I put him in bed."

"Thanks." I smiled at my sweet son. "You're good young man. I appreciate you helping. Today has been a bit hectic, and thanks for taking up the slack."

I beamed. I never noticed how much he looks like my brother Michael. His smile is very similar with large full lips that don't disappear when he smiles; his eyes have a calm sweet look but are green like his father. He has Patrick's dark hair and complexion, but most of his features come from my side of the family.

"Mase, soccer tryouts are the third week of January. Are you going out for the team?" C.J. asked.

"I'm looking forward to it."

We spent an hour or so just catching up. After a little while I leaned over and put my head on C.J.'s shoulder, and I must have fallen asleep. The next thing I knew C.J. was picking me up to put me in bed. "Sleep tight little sis, I'm glad you're back home."

----

vote please

Check out one of Mason's favorite bands Mumford and Sons...video posted

Chapter 3 - Streaking

I three words I can sum up everything I've learned about life: it goes on
-- Robert Frost

Chapter 3 - Streaking

Emily's POV:

It's gotten easier sleeping alone. Christmas has come and gone. I splurged and got myself a new bed. I no longer need to have a king size bed, if I was only sleeping in it, so I opted for a much more functional queen bed. It had been difficult sleeping in the bed I shared with Patrick when I knew he would not be there with me.

My parents and brothers have done a wonderful job filling the void Patrick left behind. We spent Christmas Eve at my parents' home at the lake, but opening presents Christmas morning was so hard...I couldn't believe Patrick was missing this.

Mason and Peyton won the jackpot when it came to gifts. My parents went a bit overboard, but this was the first time they have had my boys around during the holidays. One of Mason's favorite gifts was the matching Barcelona uniform for Peyton and him. Before lunch they were donning the uniforms with the biggest, cheesiest smiles they could muster. I know you shouldn't say this about boys-but it was soooo "sweet."

Mason is back in school. Today is the second day of tryouts. I had to have Michael pick him up yesterday, because I had a job interview. I have a call back today for a fourth grade teaching position. I am excited, but I'm more excited my boys are happy and settled in our new home.

One great thing about not having a job...I actually have time to fix breakfast for the family. My boys wander into the kitchen just as I finish cooking. I make myself a cup of Earl Grey tea...no longer the coffee drinker I once was. I've found the caffeine doesn't help with the panic feeling that has appeared since Patrick has been gone, nor does it help with my inability to sleep.

"Mason, I'll be there to pick you up after tryouts. I want to get there early enough to watch you in action."

"Ok, Mom...if it goes like it did yesterday, we don't scrimmage until about 4:15-4:30. The coach is spending the first half just working on conditioning."

After breakfast Mason catches the bus, leaving me with Peyton. Peyton helps me clear the dishes, before deciding it's time for toys. While Peyton is occupied I take a quick shower. We are going to the grocery store before I have to get ready for the interview.

Taking Peyton to the store is always fun. He has to examine all the fruit and vegetables and help me weigh each item. He also likes to show me all of his favorite things. He is very talkative during our outing, but that is ok...he is still to exploring sounds and language. By the end of our trip, Peyton was beginning to fade. It was time for an early lunch so I can get him down for a nap.

While Peyton was asleep, I changed into a purple blouse and grey pencil skirt. Patrick used to tell me that he loved the way my blue eyes sparkled when I wore purple. Breathe in - Breathe out...smile and pull myself together. "Patrick is not here. Stop thinking about him," I tell myself. I zip up my boots and then freshen my makeup. Tying my hair into a loose bun, I check my appearance in the mirror. I don't exactly look like a teacher, but that's kind of the point.

My sister-in-law offered to keep Peyton while I work ....and by 1:00 I drop Peyton off with Keira so I can go to the interview.

The interview went well. I was offered the job after I was given a tour of the school and met the other 4th grade teachers. The teacher I am replacing will be taking maternity leave in a week, and will not come back before school lets out in May. I will start work on Thursday, so I can get acquainted with the students and the teacher's schedule. I know I will make some changes after it becomes my classroom, but students need the structure that is already in place.

I feel like celebrating...I need to pick up Mason then Peyton and then maybe out for dinner.

Mason sees me arrive and gives me a quick wave. I wave back at Mason as I sit in the stands to watch the rest of today's soccer tryouts.

Foster's POV:

'Who is this kid? He's huge, and boy can he move,' I think to myself. I pick up my clip board to check his name. Cahill, Mason; 8th grade. That doesn't help. I watched him yesterday- he would be great as a mid-fielder or even a forward. Woah, look at him go...Where did he come from?'

"Cahill."

"Yes, coach," he says as he runs toward me. He looks so familiar...does he have an older brother? No he's new.... Who is he?'

"I've been watching you handle the ball. That's some nice foot work. I was thinking of putting you in as forward during practice today." He doesn't look very pleased. Most kids would jump at a chance as forward. "What position do you like?" I asked, just to see where his heart is.

"Coach, I was hoping to try my hand at keeper. Will there be a chance for me to try?"

"We can try, but I like what I see and I'm seeing you as forward." He didn't even bat an eye...he just nodded his head.

"Ok."

"By the way, I know you're new. Where were you before?"

"I just moved here from California." I was hoping he was from one of the little towns around here at least that would explain why he looks like I should know him. I swear he looks like someone I know. I guess not.

Cahill looks up in the stands and gives a quick wave to someone. I follow his eyes...it must be his older sister or something. The young lady is too old to be a girlfriend and too young to be a mom. She waves back and he takes off back across the field.

After practice the boys take off to the field house to change. "Foster, is that you?" I haven't been called Foster in like forever. I turned around, and I am met with the most amazing smile I have seen in years.

"Oh, my god...Eme? Is that my little spit fire Eme?" Standing in front of me is little Emily Frances Daniels. Wow, she looks absolutely wonderful. She has her hair tied up, but I can see it is still the dark blonde color I remember. She reaches out a hand to shake, and I shake my head back at her.

"No dear, friends don't shake...they hug." OMG, her face lit up like I had just given her a new puppy. She is so adorably beautiful. I pull her into a hug. I just want to squeeze her. "So, how long are you visiting?"

"Foster, I missed your hugs...it's so good to see you. And, I'm not visiting...I live here now."

"How long? Where?"

"I moved just before Christmas, and I'm living in neighborhood, just outside of town... Shadow Creek. C.J. lives about two blocks away."

"I noticed you waving at Cahill. Is he a friend's kid, neighbor, or something?"

"Or something. He's my son." I know my eyes must look like they would pop out of my head. She has a teenage son?

"Don't look too shocked." I shake my head at her while I run my hand through my blonde hair. "Do the math. I'm only a couple of years younger that you...I can have a 13 year old son, and I do." She says with a small chuckle. Her little laugh is so cute. I still can't believe I'm standing in front of the cutest girl I have ever met...little Emily Daniels, all grown up.

"He's only 13?" I can't believe that. I was thinking he must have been held back, he looks too big to be a 13 year old.

"Again, you don't have to look so shocked." There goes that little laugh of hers. Oh, I love that laugh.

"I was watching him during practice. I kept thinking he looked familiar. I kept trying to place him, and now, that I see you, I can see he looks a lot like your brother Michael - except the hair and eyes. Where did that come from?" I think to myself...'who did she marry? Patrick.'

"His dad," she said almost in a whisper. Her whole face drops and looks like someone just hit her in the gut. I'm not sure, but she looks like she could cry. I look down at her hands. She's twisting a wedding ring around her finger. I grab her hand and wait for her to lift her face, and then I smile.

"You look absolutely wonderful. You are still the cutest girl I've ever met." Her whole face lights up and she smiles at me. Wow, I have missed this girl.

"Why are you holding my mom's hand?" a voice said from behind me.

Mason's POV:

I'm glad soccer is over for day. I don't like playing forward. Coach said he wanted to see me in that position, but I think a more aggressive player should be there. I assisted with four goals, but I did not even have one decent shot. It's just not my scene. Hopefully, by Friday he'll start working with the keepers and give me a shot in the goal.

I turned back to look at the field just as my mom is introducing herself to the coach. She reached out her hand to meet Coach, but he grabs her and gives her a big hug...WTH. Who does he think he is? What is my mom doing hugging another guy? No, this is not good!!!!

I stop at the door of the field house to watch what they are doing. I am beyond pissed right now. Is my mom flirting with the coach? She keeps smiling and laughing like she's having a great time...Now she doing the shy "look down at your hands" move. Gaw, I can't believe her. How can she do this to my dad, or to me?

I walk across the field to put a stop to this. As I get closer my coach grabs hold of my mom's hand and just holds it while she looks at him. This makes me sick.

"Why are you holding my mom's hand?" I hope my voice sounds as angry as I am feeling. My mom immediately drops the coach's hand, and takes a step away from him.

"Cahill, nice work today. I was just talking to your mom." He reaches out and takes my mom's hand again, and turns around to face me. "I had no idea this was your mother. I've loved this girl for most of my life." WTH. I look from one to the other. How can they look so happy with themselves while they rip my life apart?

"She's had a place in my heart since she came running through my living room with nothing on but panties and a smile." I clinch my fist. I don't care that this man is my soccer coach, I'm ready to take him out.

"Foster, you better tell him the rest of the story. He doesn't look too happy with you." Damn right I'm not happy.

"I met your mother when I was 5 years old...that would make you what about 2 ½ or 3."

"Sounds right."

"Her grandmother lived down from my parents. Your uncles used to come over a play when they were visiting. Well, how do I say this?" He pauses. Just get on with it already. "Your mother was not fond of wearing clothes back then." I look at my mom as she turns a bright shade of pink. "She ran away from her grandmother to go find Michael and C.J. who were at my house. We were all in the living room playing with Hot Wheels, and the next thing I knew there was a sweet little blonde cutie pie running through my house with nothing on but panties." We all laugh at the thought of my mother streaking through the living room being chased by my great-grandmother. Come to find out my great-grandmother was not too happy with the unladylike behavior, and my mother got a bit of a fly-swatter on her behind as a punishment.

After the story I smile and kiss my mom's cheek. I'm still a bit worried about how comfortable Coach is with my mom, but my mom doesn't look like she interested in him. She looks like she has a friend. She nudges Coach in the shoulder and told him to behave and stop embarrassing her. She even threatens to sic Uncle Michael on him.

"How did it go?" I asked about her interview. "I got it," she says with a big smile.

"How did what go, and what did you get?" Coach asked her.

She tells him about her new job. I'm happy for my mom. I'm glad she got a job.

"I think this calls for a celebration," she tells me. "How about we go get some pizza and a movie?" I agree, and then she turns to Coach Foster and asks him to join us.

"I'd love to, but can I bring my best girl with me?" Yeah, he has a girlfriend... he needs to remember that and leave my mom alone.

Emily's POV:

It's great to see my friend. I have missed Foster. He always knew how to make me smile.

"Foster, would you like to join us?" I am surprised when he agreed. He has the most comforting smile and soft brown eyes.

"I'd love to, but can I bring my best girl with me?" I should have known that Foster would not be single. He's too good looking not to catch the eye of some special lady. I smile at him and tell him to bring whomever he wants.

After leaving Foster, I want to pick up pizza and collect Peyton. This has turned out to be a great day...

----

please vote

Check out Foster...I posted a picture of the perfect Will Foster

Chapter 4 - You're Married?

R are is true love, true friendship is rarer -- Jean de La Fontaine

Chapter 4 - Married?

Emily's POV:

I order pizza while Mason runs back to the field house to change. I make plans for Foster to join us at 6:00. Pizza, movie and good company...what a way to spend the evening.

Mason and I discuss movie choices as we pick up pizza and Peyton. We narrow it down to Thor or Green-Lantern, so he's going to surprise me.

Mason puts the pizza on the kitchen island, and returns to the car to collect all of his soccer gear and backpack. I carry Peyton in the house and steal a few hugs, while I wipe off the counter to prepare for our makeshift pizza buffet.

Within 5 minutes, the doorbell rang. Instead of Foster and his lady-friend, I was greeted by Foster and two lovely young ladies (girls). The taller girl has light brown hair and her daddy's milk chocolate eyes. There is little doubt that she belongs to Will Foster. She looks like she is about Mason's age and she is beautiful. The smaller girl is probably in 3 or 4 grade with very curly blonde hair and the most intense sage green eyes. Like the taller girl she is also beautiful. I look at her light complexion, pink lips and cheeks, and her eyes...I can tell these girls are not genetically related to each other.

"Sorry, I should have called to let you know we had an extra guest, but I didn't have your number." He turns his gaze to the girls. "This is my best girl - my daughter Chandler," gesturing toward the taller brown-eyed girl. "And, this is our friend Addyson. We call her Addy." The little blonde girl beams at me. Chandler is a bit shy or nervous, but little Miss Addy looks like she has a million questions just ready to burst out of her mouth. I reach out my hand and introduce myself. "And who do we have here," he asks looking at Peyton, who is still in my arms.

"Oh, sorry...this is my son Peyton. He's almost two."

The look of shock on Foster's face was priceless. "Yes, he was on purpose," answering the unasked question. He chuckles at my response. He asked if other people have ever been bold enough to ask that out loud. I told him no, but I can always see the question on their faces.

I walk with our guests to the living room and do a quick introduction to Mason. Putting Peyton down, I head to the kitchen with Foster and gather plates, napkins, and drinks for dinner. The older kids all help themselves to pizza before gathering back into the living room for the movie.

Mason chose to watch Brave instead of a superhero movie. He thought it would be a better choice considering the audience. He was correct, and I smile at his decision.

Foster and I sit on the couch. Mason and Peyton have a picnic blanket spread out for the kids to sit and eat. "Are you dating my Uncle Will?"

Addyson asked. I choke on the bluntness of the young girl. This question got the attention of Mason and Chandler. Then, I chuckle and look at Foster who is finding this situation amusing.

"No, your 'uncle' and I are not dating," I heard both the both older children breath in relief. Addy just smiled and looked like she had more to ask, so I offered a chance to ask me two more questions.

"You have a wedding ring on, Are you married?"

"Yes, sweety, I am." Mason gives me a quizzical look.

"Then, where's your husband? And does he know you have Uncle Will here?" I feel a huge pain in my heart. I take a deep breath and try to recover, as Foster looks at me with concerning eyes. I smile at the little girl who did nothing, but ask the question most everyone else has asked in the past 3 ½ months.

"Oh, sweety...that was more than two questions." I get up to grab the dirty dishes and carry them to the kitchen. Foster's phone rings and he steps in the other room to answer.

He finds me in the kitchen and puts a hand on my shoulder and looks out the window. "Do you want to talk about it?"

"Not today."

"Ok, I'm here when you're ready. " He smiled at me and gave me a gentle hug.

"I doubt it will be anytime soon."

He smiled and gave me a little wink. "Well, get comfortable. I just got you back in my life...You're not getting rid of me." He assessed my face and added, "You need a friend, and I am a good friend. "

"Cooper is on his way to pick up Addy."

He moves his hand gently from my shoulder and rubs it up and down on my back. It's a small gesture that is very comforting. I breathe in and smell the scent that is uniquely Foster. I start to pull away as Addy runs into the kitchen holding her leg showing me a small cut that is in the process of healing. She asks for a new band-aid. I barely get her situated on the counter to assess her need, when the door bell rang.

"I'll get that," Foster says as he leaves the kitchen.

After cleaning her cut leg, I apply a new band aid. She was not too impressed with the choices of Cars, superheroes, and sport decorated bandages. She decided on sports so she could look tough. As we finish, I look up and meet the most beautiful man I have ever seen. For a moment I thought he was mirroring my look or something, but then I saw it was more like curiosity...then anger.

"I was just cleaning up her leg. She has a cut that is healing, and she needed a new bandage. I'm sorry. She wasn't hurt here. She has only been watching a movie with Chandler and my sons." I rambled, not knowing why he was looking at me like that. My words are not eloquent, but he makes me nervous. I turn away from his glare and look at Foster for comfort.

Cooper's POV:

"Hey man, I'm on my way over to pick up Addy. Thanks for taking care of her." This is the 2nd time this week Will has had to bail me out. I need to find a new driver soon. I've been short handed for almost a month. It wasn't bad, but with construction picking back up. I have to spend too much time at work and away from Addy. Mills Lumber has seen a boom in business lately, and I need to hire more staff soon.

"I'm not home," Will says.

"That's ok. Where can I meet you?"

"Actually, I'm already in your neighborhood." He gives me the address, and it's just a couple of streets over from my house.

"I'll be there in less than 10."

As I pull onto the street, I see Will's truck in the driveway of a new house. I didn't even know the house was occupied, yet. I've been working so much, I didn't even notice that a new family moved in. I get out of my BMW x5 and walk up to the front door. I see Will through the window hugging a woman...they look very cozy.

I sometimes wonder about my friend. For being such a great guy, he has terrible taste in women. I hope this one is better than the last chick he was with, but even she was better than that ex-wife of his.

Will opens the front door and invites me in the house. I follow him to the kitchen where I see my niece sitting on the counter. I watch as she gets her knee bandaged by the lady that was hugging Will. The lady hovering over her and doctoring her knee looks at her with such kindness. She smiles down at my niece, and then she looks up and meets my eyes. I am stunned, breathless. She has the most beautiful kind face I have ever seen. Her eyes are the most beautiful bright blue, and she is showing such gentleness to Addy...but she is with Will. If her personality matches her face, Will is one lucky son of a gun.

She smiles at me. Then, she looks, I don't know nervous. "I was just cleaning up her leg. She has a cut that is healing, and she needed a new bandage. I'm sorry. She wasn't hurt here. She has only been watching a movie with Chandler and my sons." Now she looks scared and turns her gaze toward Will. He gives a half smile and folds her into his arms like she belongs to him, and she seems to melt into his arms.

"This is Emily...?" He looks at her, enjoying a little moment.

"Cahill," she says. He's quite cozy with this woman he just met.

"Emily this is my friend Cooper Mills...Addy's uncle." Will happily introduces us. She pulls away from him and smiles at me in a timid way, and told me it was nice to meet me. She let me know how wonderful she thought Addy was. I told her she is a bit precocious and she agreed as we both laughed. She has a nice warm laugh, but her happiness didn't quite meet her eyes. They looked a bit sad.

Will offered me pizza, and we stood in the kitchen talking. Now I know why he didn't know her last name. I was told how Will and Emily knew each other, about how he took her to her senior prom, and how they found each other today. They also told me why she keeps calling Will by his last name. They seem too happy and comfortable together... I am a bit jealous.

I guess she must have been the one that got away. As we stood talking I couldn't help but notice the big rock on her finger. She's married. Is she cheating on her husband with Will? Is he out of his mind? No matter how sweet she is...she is married and a cheater. I can't help but feel sick to my stomach...I glare at her and then to Will. He ignores me and looks at her adoringly...she on the other hand gets it. Her demeanor changes. Good at least she has a conscious.

She broke eye contact with me as a little boy came running into the kitchen, wanting to be held. "Let me hold you," he told her. She picks him up and he snuggles into her neck. It was a sweet sight that was not missed by Will. What is he thinking?

I hear a small commotion and then I am greeted my Michael Daniels. I don't even remember hearing the knock or the doorbell. He is standing by a very tall, slim young man who looks a lot like him. I didn't even know he had a kid.

The young man asked, "Mom, can I get some more soda?" That was her son. She doesn't look old enough to have a kid that big. He is only a few inches shorter than Michael. He looks about 16 or so. Maybe this is her stepson. She answered him and he gladly poured himself something to drink.

"Son, how was tryouts?" Michael asked. Son? That's his kid with this woman?

"They went fine...I think. You need to ask Coach." He answered as he looked at Will.

Will proceeds to tell him about how practice went today. Obviously he was there for yesterday's tryout. As they are talking, the little boy in Emily's arms practically leaps out of her arms into Michael's. "Hey there little man." He takes the kid and proceeds to kiss Emily on the temple. She smiles at him in a way that almost reaches her eyes. I can tell she loves this man. Will, WTH? Is Will actually watching what is going on...what is he thinking?

Michael takes Emily's hand and touches her wedding ring, and gives her a sad smile...she returns with a nod. He shakes his head at her and looks questioningly at me and Will. She looks away from him stares at the floor. This whole silent conversation tells me that there is a lot going on here... Will doesn't need to get in the middle of this.

The little boy in Michael's arms seems very comfortable. "I'm going to take him to get his pjs, if that is ok with you? You stay here and enjoy your company." She said thank you to him as he left the room. Does he live here?

It dawned on me that this is the house that Michael was building, and in such a hurry to finish. I guess I know why now. It was for himself. As long as I have known Michael through business...I never knew he was married.

Emily's POV:

I feel like I'm being judged. I can't help but feel I'm under a microscope. Thank goodness Foster is here with me. He smiles at me just like when we were kids. He always knew how to make me feel comfortable. Even though I was not usually awkward in social situations, Foster has always made me feel at home with him. He is the nicest, funniest guy I know. His friend on the other hand makes me feel uncomfortable. He smiles one minute and glares the next.

Peyton comes in with his standard "let me hold you" line and I pick him up. He is a bit sleepy. I need to excuse myself and get him ready for bed. Just as I was about to leave the room, my brother Michael come to the kitchen. Mason came in to get more soda, and Peyton practically jumped out of my arm into Michael's.

After talking to Mason and Foster about tryouts, he left to put Peyton to bed for me. Michael returns a few minutes later and lets me know he put Peyton in bed and he was already asleep. I give him quick hug and thank him.

"So, how did it go today?" He asked about my job interview.

"Great. I got the job. I start Thursday. I shadow the teacher for two days, but I am officially teaching 4th grade on Monday. I'll be there until the end of the year. Then, I may have to interview again for a permanent position for next year."

He was so excited that he picked me up a twirled me around in circles. Foster laughed, but I can feel Cooper glaring at me...I try to ignore him.

"That's great!!!" He grabs my hand and for the second time tonight he touches my wedding ring. Then, he motioned toward Foster with a questioning look...I shook my head no. I'm sure if he was asking if I was interested in Foster or if I told Foster about Patrick...either way the answer was no. It's too soon for me to think about being with someone else even if it is

Foster. He must know that Patrick is one subject I don't talk about...with anyone.

He looked a little sad at my answer.

After a while Cooper left with Addy and Foster and my brother were saying their goodbyes as I was cleaning up our mess in the kitchen. All in all it was a good night.

Michael's POV:

"Foster, do you have a minute?" I asked him as we left the house. His daughter was already in his truck.

"Sure, what do you need?"

"What's going on with Emily?"

"Nothing, we saw each other after tryouts. She invited me over to celebrate her new job. Nothing more."

"What about you?"

"Friends, just like always."

"Good. She needs a friend right now."

"I love your sister...you know that...I won't hurt her. What happened with Patrick? She kind of gets weird if she hears his name."

"Honestly, I'd love to tell you, but I'm waiting for her to talk. It's a 'no-go' conversation for her.

"That's why I wanted to talk with you. It's been over 3 months, and she still won't speak about him. I know she's hurting, she's angry, and she's trying to keep it all together. She seems to be happy to see you."

"Thanks...she makes me happy...she always has."

"C.J. and I can't be with her all the time. She's wound up tight, and I'm scared she's going to burst."

"I'll be here for her. Always...is there anything I need to know?"

I meet his questioning eyes and shake my head.

----

please vote

Check out Cooper...I've posted a picture of a perfect Cooper Mills.

Chapter 5 - You're back

D o all you can to make your dreams come true -- Joel Osteen

Chapter 5

Emily POV:

I stretch, roll over, and open my eyes. Patrick is sitting on my bed studying me. He smiles at me and then he reaches out and caresses my face. "I'm sorry I didn't mean to wake you up." His eyes darken and are very full of desire. "I've missed you, sweetheart," he tells me.

"I can't believe you're here. I wasn't expecting you...I'm glad you're back. How was your flight? When did you get in?" He stands and begins unbuttoning his shirt. I can't help but watch as he begins to reveal his body to me. It's been too long. I feel the familiar ache I have for him.

"I just got here." I watch him in the dim light as he finishes undressing and joins me under the blankets. "I love you Patrick. I've really missed you," I tell him as his hand begins to find my skin under my night gown. I miss his touch, his smell, and him. I raise my hands over my head and enjoy his touch. All of the months of absence seem to evaporate as his touch melts into my skin. I can't believe he's back.

"Oh god, Em - your skin feels so good." With one hand rubbing my back under my nightshirt and the other caressing my cheek, my body begins to burn...I have missed him - missed this. "You are so beautiful...I love you, Em. I don't ever want to be that far away from you again. These past few months have been the worst." He leans forward gently to kiss my lips. I watch his eyes darken and heat surges through my body. As our lips meet I move my hand to his hair...

I wake up in a cold sweat. Breathe! I keep having the same reoccurring dreams, each of them about Patrick returning. Breathe in...breathe...out... It's getting harder to sleep. I thought with time it would become easier, but it's not.

It's Friday the last day of soccer tryouts. Foster tells Mason that he made the team, but he is still waiting to find out what position he will be playing. It's been over a week since I have celebrated my new job. I was actually shocked on the first day of work, seeing Addyson sitting all sweet faced in my new classroom.

I stand and stretch. It's only 3:45 a.m., but there is no way I can go back to sleep. My heart hurts. This dream felt so real. I need to do something so I can quit thinking about Patrick.

By 5:00 I have done two loads of laundry, cleaned the kitchen and made my bed. I still have a lot of nervous energy... I change clothes, put on my running shoes, and grab my iPod and mace (because my mom didn't raise a fool). I leave a note for Mason, in case he gets up before I get back home. I head off to the walking track that is lit with path lights. I need to clear my head...I hope this helps.

I pick up my pace as the song changes to One More Night by Maroon 5 a much more upbeat rhythm. As I am almost half way around the track, I am aware of movement behind me. I put my hands on my can of mace and pick up my pace a bit more. I turn down my music so I can concentrate on my surroundings. The sound of footsteps behind me starts to increase and move closer. Fear is beginning to overwhelm me. I'm still about half a track length away from the path to my house. As I try to calm my fears and concentrate on the exit, I feel a hand touch my arm. I pull the mace and aim it at the intruder.

"What the Hell! You could have been maced. Don't ever sneak up on someone like that. You scared me." I am fuming. I stop to catch my breath. Relief takes over my body and suddenly I am exhausted. I collapse onto the track still shaken. He bends down to look at my face.

"I'm sorry...what are you doing out here at this time of day...alone?" He gives me the same look as he did the other day something between a glare and contempt. I try to shake it off. I get up and begin walking without saying a word to him.

"You didn't answer my question," he says. I try to ignore him, but he begins to walk beside me. After a bit of silence he asks, "Does your husband know you're out here alone?"

"You're here with me...I am not alone anymore," I say with as much con-tempt as his face shows me. How dare he bring up Patrick! Of course Patrick doesn't know I'm here alone, he doesn't know anything that is hap-pening in my life. Suddenly I am overwhelmed with thoughts of Patrick and the dream that woke me early this morning. I try to blink back the tears that are starting to prick my eyes. "To answer your question, No, my husband doesn't know I'm out here running."

"So, you are married?" I look away, not wanting to explain myself to him. I don't see that it is any of his business. "What about Will? Are you keeping him as a piece on the side, while you build a life with Michael?"

"What are you talking about? Michael is my brother, and Will is my friend that's it." So, that was his problem. He thought I was cheating on my husband with Foster, and to top it off he thought Michael was my husband. What an idiot!

"So, where's your husband?" Will he never stop with the judgmental attitude? I'm livid!!!! I shake my head at him and look away from his glaring eyes...I'm out of here. I pick up my pace and cut through the woods to my house. Cooper follows me.

"I'm sorry." His eyes actually look like he means it. "I just don't want to see my friend hurt."

"He's my friend, too. I don't want to see him hurt, either. If you are worried about this...I would never hurt him. Are we good now?" He smiles at me, and can't help but look at his beautiful blue eyes. He seems to trying to read my intensions. I smile at him, and his face brightens and I can't believe how absolutely stunning he is... My thoughts immediately turn to Patrick...breathe.

"Thanks, that's what I needed to know. Do me a favor...next time you decide to go running early in the morning, call me. I'll go with you. Will wouldn't like the idea of you being out by yourself at this hour, and neither do I." He gives me his phone number, excuses himself and heads back toward his house.

As I open the door, a very unusual sight greets me. Mason is playing a downhill skiing game on the wii. He is holding Peyton in his arms face forward. They lean forward like they are headed downhill, and then they pull upright...as Peyton squeals, "Do again!" I chuckle at the sight. My boys are the only reminder I need, and I need to remember that I am blessed.

"How long have you been up?" I ask.

"About 20 minutes. Peyton wanted to play. I hope that is ok. How was your run?"

"It was good...1 full lap. Not bad for a beginner." The path is just over a mile and a half encircling a rather large oblong open field and small park.

"Mom, pretty soon you'll be ready for a 10K or a half marathon. That's not bad at all." Mason smiles and encourages.

I love my new job. One of the biggest blessings are my new co-workers. At my last job I had friends, but the staff was not as warm and inviting as this one was. The first person I met was Lillian Johnson, or Lil.

She's only a few years younger than my mother. We hit it off quickly...d efinitely when we found out that we both knew a lot of the same people. Our first day, we play gossip catch-up, and she could really dish the dirt - she is very much the informer. I think I now know what has happened to everyone in my graduating class. To say she has a personality would be an understatement. She most definitely will live life to the very last moment...while playing mother hen to all who are around her.

There are a couple of younger teachers fresh out of college that has bonded with Lil. She seems to be their mother protector, and since I'm new to the staff, she has brought me under her wing. I think I'm a bit more conservative in my actions than these ladies, but they don't seem to hold that against me. They are a lot of fun to be around. There hasn't been a dull moment, yet. At this rate there may never be.

We all have lunch at the same time, and Lil strictly enforces the "no class-room talk" zone... that means we don't discuss school or work. It's nice to have adult conversation when your day is usually completely filled with children. The ladies discussed plans for an upcoming 'girlfriend' night. Once a month they plan a day or night out. The last one consisted of a daylong shopping trip to Memphis. By the sounds of it, the younger teachers act like teenagers and Lil plays along with them. Even though I am part of the discussion, I feel like an observer for most of it because of the close bonds of these ladies.

When lunch is over I go to pick up my students from the cafeteria. To my surprise Cooper Mills is sitting at a side table eating lunch with Addy. Seeing him again today catches me a bit off guard. He look up at me and I feel my face warm. Seriously, did I just blush when he looked at me?

"Mr. Mills, nice to see you. Did you enjoy your lunch with Addy?" I ask as I approach the table. He gives me a discerning look and tells me I could call him Cooper. On Fridays, whenever he can, he eats lunch with Addy. Sometimes he eats at school and other times he will check her out and take her to lunch.

As I am gathering my students, Cooper comes over to talk to me. "I was serious this morning. I don't like the idea you were out by yourself so early in the morning. Next time call me. I'm usually up by 5:00." He hands me a piece of paper with his phone number. "I wasn't sure if you remembered my number when I told you earlier. Now you have it written down. Please don't go alone."

I look directly at his face to thank him. His eyes never leave mine as he gives me a half smile. "Thank you," I say. I feel heat rising to my face. Seriously, blushing again? WTH!

After he leaves, the rest of the day flows without a hitch. I am looking forward to catch the last day of Mason's tryout. Mason is nervous that he will only be playing on the field. He might be a little disappointed if he doesn't get a chance in the goal.

When I am leaving school, I notice Addy sitting in the office. "Why are you in here?" I ask.

"It seems like Amy forgot that she had to pick me up today."

"Oh, let's call your mom and see when she can come get you."

"I don't have a mom." With those simple words my heart stops. I try not to be affected by what she has said.

"Ok, let's call your uncle and see if he can help."

I pull out the paper with his Cooper's phone number, and call him. "Hello, Mr. Mills this is Ms. Cahill," I say when he answers. Not feeling comfortable enough to call him by his first name, yet.

"Cooper, please. What can I do for you?"

"I have Addy with me. She was expecting someone named Amy to come get her from school, but she hasn't arrived. Do you know anything about how she gets home, if Amy doesn't come?"

"I'm sorry. Let me call Amy and see what is keeping her. I will call you back on this number in just a few moments." After I hang up with Cooper, I look over at Addy. She smiles at me waiting to hear what her Uncle Cooper says.

"To answer your question. If Amy doesn't come get me then Uncle Will or Uncle Cooper comes. I live with Uncle Cooper. No one else has ever picked me up since my mother died." I knew her Uncle Will couldn't come because he has soccer tryouts. I guess Uncle Cooper will be coming to the rescue. My phone rang and it was Cooper calling me back.

"Emily, can I call you Emily?"

"Yes."

"Amy is stuck behind a wreck on I-40 and won't be able to get there for another hour. She had left a message for me at work, but I haven't been back to the office, yet. I'm just now heading back to town. I can be there in 30 minutes."

"If it's ok with you, why don't I take her with me and I'll drop her off at your house or work on my way home?"

"I don't want to be a bother."

"It's not a problem, she can keep me company for a while."

"I do appreciate it." Cooper asks me to bring her by the store after I pick up Mason. Addy beams when I tell her that she would be spending the rest of the afternoon with me. She could hardly contain her excitement about hangin' with the teacher.

We sit in the stands to watch the boy's soccer team. Addy is full of nervous energy, and begins to ramble about any and every thing that she was thinking. I learned that she lives with her Uncle Cooper because he is her only family, that both of her parents are dead, that she only lost her mom this past year, and that she thinks her Uncle Will likes me. She holds nothing back, and is very blunt with her information. I chuckle at some of the randomness of her conversation. It reminds me of the saying 'out of the mouth of babes'-brutal honesty.

When the boys are finishing up on the field, Foster calls them all over to talk to the team. From the reaction of Mason he must have been told he could play keeper (goalie). He looks over to me in the stands with the largest smile on his face, and he gives me a fist. I air fist bump him and he turns back to Foster to hear about practice dates. The boys are dismissed and Addy takes off to the field and barrels into Foster. He picks her up and throws her over his shoulder like she was a sack of potatoes, and she erupts in giggles.

"Where's Cooper?" he asks her, and she explains how she gets to hang out with her teacher. Then, she twists around in his arms to whisper in his ear. A shocked look lands on his face as our eyes met. He puts Addy down and she runs off to the door of the field house.

"Ok, what was that about?" I have to ask.

"She was busy playing matchmaker. I think she approves of you. She says you're very pretty and nice, too." He shakes his head and looks a bit embarrassed. "But then again, I've always known that," he says and winks at me. I look around to check on Addy, and she is sitting watching Foster and me. She seams very pleased with herself.

Chandler walks over after track practice and sits down next to Addy with her gym bag and glares at Foster, and then at me. I take a small step away from Foster to make sure Chandler understands that I am his friend not a girlfriend. She gives me a small smile.

Foster clears his throat to get my attention. "Don't let Chandler scare you. She likes you...she told me so."

After a few minutes we are joined by Mason, followed closely by Chandler and Addy. "Did you tell her?" Mason asks Foster.

"No, I left that for you."

"Coach Foster is letting me play keeper. Zac is the starter, but he will let me sub in."

"Eme, he's good, but what's better he is highly motivated. If he was able to get some extra training, he could be great. I know a few people that help train goalies. Let me talk to them about helping him." He gives Mason a small pat on the back. "Good job kid."

"Let me know, we'll work it out." Mason did a small cheer and turns back toward the girls. I thank Foster for giving Mason a chance, and let him know how much this means to him.

We leave Foster and Chandler and head to the car, when my phone begins to ring. "Cooper, I was just about to call you. I'm leaving now on my to the store with Addy," I say as I unlock the vehicle and Mason puts his equipment in the trunk.

"I'm glad I was able to catch you. I meeting with some contractors, and I'm headed out to a job site. Could you check with Will and see if he can keep Addy for me?" I agree to check and hang up.

Catching up with Foster, "Cooper needs to know if you can watch Addy until he gets back from a job site."

"I can't, I have a date," he tells me. He smiles at me weakly, and I return his smile with one that I hoped looked much happier than his.

"It's ok. I'll call him back let him know she can stay with me. Have fun," I say and he reaches out for my hand. I give his a small squeeze and leave.

As I return to the car, I call Cooper to let him know of Will's plans. Before he could worry about what to do, I offer to keep Addy with me. He doesn't have to worry. He can finish his work, and then come get Addy.

Addy walks with me over to pick up Peyton from Keira's house. Peyton is overjoyed to see Addy again. She likes pushing his stroller for me. I think she is trying to play momma to my little man. She talks to him about his day, his toys, and anything else that pops into her head. Peyton loves the attention.

When we return to the house, Addy stays with me instead of heading off to play with the boys; in the kitchen she helps (watches) me cook. I can tell she misses her mother by how she craves affection from a woman. "Would like to learn how to cook?" and she nods her head. Mason had asked to have salmon (his favorite) for dinner. Addy helps me cut vegetables and prepare a pan for the salmon. She is by my side during the whole prep, and I smile at her and ask, "Were you always this helpful with your mom?"

"No, not really. She was sick for a long time, and she wasn't able to cook much. Mostly she just laid around, but I do like to help my Uncle Cooper."

"I'm sure he likes the help." Finish the preparing dinner and she helps set the table. We add a place for Cooper just in case he finishes work in time to join us. As we sit down to dinner, the doorbell rings.

"Cooper," I greet him at the door. "We were just sitting down for dinner. Would you like to join us?" He trys to make an excuse, but in the end with Addy's persuasion, he accepts my invitation.

Cooper's POV:

I'm beat. I need to get Addy home, fed, and in bed. This has been a long week, and it probably won't slow down this weekend either. I usually don't even go into work on Saturday, but I will have to tomorrow just to catch up. That's not even taking in the extra work this new project will be sending me. I like that my business here has taken off, but Addy is my primary concern here. How can I be what she needs, hell what my sister need me to be, if I spend all my time working.

When Emily called to let me know Addy was still at school, it was just another reminder of how I was failing as her guardian. I need to let Emily know how grateful I am that she was willing to help me with Addy. She probably only helped me out because Addy is her student, or that Will is her friend. Still, it was nice to have help. Just thinking about how sweet she was on the phone make me smile. Will sure knew what he was doing when he picked her.

She answered the door and the smell from the kitchen made my mouth water. "Mr...um, Cooper," our eyes met and my throat closed. Every time I saw her today, I the same reaction. I swallowed hard preparing to speak and ask for Addy. "We were just sitting down for dinner. Would you like to join us?" She smiled at me. I need to get out of here.

I shake my head. "No thank you...I need to be going. Is Addy ready?"

Addy came barreling around the corner, "Uncle Cooper, I helped make dinner, and it's really good. You need to come get some." I tilted my head up to see Emily's face. She was no longer looking at me; she was Addy and all of her excitement. Ok, that's better. I can stay as long as I can keep my distance from Emily. I can do this for Addy.

"Ok, I'd love to stay."

Emily raised her eyebrows at me and headed back to the dinner table. She sat down by Peyton who was in his booster seat, and Addy sat down beside her. I noticed they had set the table expecting me to stay and eat. "We were hoping you would join us," Emily said. "What would you like to drink?" she asked as she was pushing her chair back to stand. She began naming drink possibilities.

"How about I follow you and choose something?" I followed her into the kitchen.

"Thank you for today. I needed help with Addy. Thank you." She nodded and smiled as our eyes met, she blushed. She had done that earlier today. Oh god, that's beautiful.

She quickly fixes me a drink, and we head back to the table.

Emily asked, "What was the best part of your day?" Each child had an opportunity to answer. As we ate dinner Mason talked about soccer, Addy talked about any/every thing, and Peyton talked to just hear his voice. At times it was a bit noisy, but it was comforting. As I pondered the question I would have to say "Emily", because she was there through my whole day. She was by far the best part of today.

After dinner I helped Emily clean the table. I wasn't ready to leave, so I agreed to stay when Addy and Mason wanted to start a movie. Peyton was sitting comfortably between Emily and me. He was a bit active, but for his age he was not so bad.

"I think my little man is getting tired. I'm going to get him ready for bed. I'll be right back."

When she returned to her spot on the couch, Peyton took up residence in her arms. She spent some time just watching at him as his eyes flutter. He nestled himself in her arms and faded off to sleep. She smiled up at me and excused herself to put Peyton to bed. I'm not sure where her husband is, but what kind of man would leave all of this...her, his family and her.

I got up to get a drink of water and Emily found me in the kitchen. "What is your husband's name?" I asked her. This was the first time she didn't flinch when I asked a personal question.

"His name is Patrick."

"Well, he's a lucky man."

"Thank you." She whispered her response and looked away from me. I can only see pain, and maybe a bit of anger.

I quickly took the hint that this is not a subject for conversation. Emily and I sat at the kitchen island, and talked for the next hour or so about kids, work, interests, and... She has a very easy manner. She let me vent about needing more help at work, and learning the ropes of being a single parent. She was a good listener, easy to talk to, and very easy to look at.

I keep drifting off from the words she spoke and watching her talk. I want to reach out and touch her, but I couldn't do that. My mind keeps traveling to thoughts that I should not be thinking about a married woman, and Will's female friend. If I were to touch her, I'm not sure my thoughts would remain only thoughts.

It was getting late and I needed to Addy home. At the door Addy bear hugged Emily, "I'll see you on Monday. I'm glad I was able to spend my day with you." Emily's word reached the heart of my niece.

"Goodnight, Emily. Thank you for dinner. I had a very nice evening," I watched as her smile reached her eyes, and my heart skipped a beat. "Please do me a favor, I don't like that your are out early in the morning running alone, call me or someone else to go with you. Even though this is a safe neighborhood, you shouldn't go alone."

"What? You don't think I can take care of myself?"

"Yes, I do...but if something happened to you I would forgive myself, and Will would never forgive me."

"Fine, I'll call you if I feel the need to run early in the morning again."

"Thank you, goodnight."

"Goodnight."

Please vote and/or comment your feedback is important to me.

A song by Howie Day has been posted. It had been playing in the background of my head as I wrote this chapter.

Chapter 6 - Let's Fix You

A single twig breaks, but the bundle of twigs is strong.--Tecumseh

Chapter 6 - Let's Fix You

Foster's POV:

"Cahill, Come here a minute."

I need to find out what's going on with Emily. After talking with Michael yesterday, I'm concerned how she's doing mentally. I have seen her almost every day since soccer season started. Between seeing her for a bit after practice and lunch on Sundays at her grandmother's house, I've seen her a lot. And yet she has been hiding from me at the same time. Maybe I've had my head stuck up my own ass, which was what it felt like when Michael told me what he has observed. Am I such a dick, so wrapped up in myself that I didn't notice? I guess that would be a yes. Well, not anymore. She is definitely on my radar, now.

"Yeah, Coach what do you need?"

"How are things at home?"

"I don't know what you mean, sir." This kid is almost as tall as I am and he is standing there staring at my nose, then my forehead. He is avoiding looking me in the eyes. Oh, Emily...

"I'm talking to you as your Coach or your mom's friend, whichever makes this conversation easier for you." I get a quizzical look from him. "I talked with your Uncle Michael. He's worried about your mom. Has he talked with you?"

"No sir, he hasn't talked to me about my mom in a while. We mostly talk about school and soccer. What's wrong with my mom?"

"That's what I'm trying to find out. How are things at home? How is your mom doing?"

He hangs his head and looks bit lost in his thoughts. "I don't know what you want me to tell you." He is a bit angry. I adjust my stance so he doesn't see me as a threat. He needs to trust that I'm here to help him and his mom. "She doesn't sleep. She thinks I don't know, but I do. Is that what you want to know?

"Yeah, that and anything else you want to get off your chest. How long has this been going on?"

"A few weeks maybe four...she leaves early in the morning if it's not raining. She sometimes is gone for close to an hour or so." I saw anger in his face, he couldn't mask it.

"What else? I see it on your face. What's bothering you?"

"I think she is seeing someone." I smile. I'm happy for her, but the way Mason looks as he bites out his words, he is pissed.

"This may hurt a little, but she and your dad are no longer together. Were you hoping that they would get back together?"

"That will NEVER happen!" Anger - big anger. I stay calm. Pushing an angry teenage boy will not help anyone. I give him a moment to collect himself before I proceed.

"Have you talked to anyone about what happened with your mom and dad?" He shakes his head at me. "Maybe it's time to get it off your chest."

"What about practice, Coach."

"Coach White is running drills and will start practice without me if I don't show up. You need to clear your head before you take the field. You're no good to yourself or the team right now."

Mason lets out a large breath and began. Within the first few words every-thing changes. I know Mason and I will not make it to the practice field.

Mason let the words flow through his body in a steady stream of memories. He stares at the wall as his words pour out of his thoughts and heart. I don't touch him...I don't move...worried that any movement will shut him up and shut him down. He talks about that day in October with almost no emotion. He isn't sad, or angry, or happy, or anything...numb would best describe the boy in front of me. That was not good.

"Am I the first person you've talked to about all of this?"

"Yeah, I can't talk to mom. She's dealing with this and her own problems." Emily you have a great boy I think as I listened to Mason.

"You can come to me whenever you want. Your mom and I have always been friends. I'm not going anywhere." Oh god, I want to keep that promise to him. "You also have to know you have Michael and CJ...shit boy , you have more family that I can count."

By the time Mason and I finish talking the team was coming back in from practice. Emily stands at the doorway, worried about her son and why he wasn't on the field. She can tell by the grim faces that met hers that I knew all of the things she hasn't been able to say.

My hands are on the phone texting Michael and Cooper, as I watch Mason walk over to talk to his mom. Michael is on his way to pick up Mason and take care of the boys for Emily, and Cooper will be taking care of Chandler for me. I need to be here for Emily.

I reach over and take her hand letting her know I'm here. "You're withering away. You're not blooming - you're no longer the same girl I saw just a month ago. I'm just sorry I didn't notice it earlier, but I see it now." She gives me a half-hearted smile. "You'll get through this...I've got you.

For the life of me I can't figure out where she got stuck...denial or an ger...but from looking at her now...I think depression. Even though she looks amazing, I can see the darker circles under her eyes she is hiding with makeup. I think she must have lost a few pounds over the last few weeks; her clothes seem to be hanging on her. She didn't have enough extra to loose.

Everyone had leaves the field house for the evening, letting Mason, Emily and me to talk. "Tell me what's going on with you. I don't mean with Patrick. Mason filled me in on that."

Mason hangs his head before looking up at his mom. She brushes his hair back off of his forehead and nods at him. She isn't angry or upset, and this is her way of letting him know. "I'm glad he was able to talk to someone. It worries me that he hasn't talked about any of this with anyone."

"Neither have you, mom."

"I will when I'm ready."

"I want you to know that you have a great son. He worries about you just like you worry about him. Most boys don't care about much outside of their own self." She smiles up at her son. "I'm also worried about you-here and now- How are you doing?"

"Don't worry about me, I'm fine." Panic and exhaustion is written all over her face; I can see her hallow eyes; her pallor is also an issue...she looks ill compared to just a month ago.

"Em, it's me. You're not fine. Talk to me."

"What do you want me to say," she spat out in anger. I look around the room to make sure we are completely alone. The coast is clear...let her rip. "That some days everything is fine and dandy, and then reality sets in and I get so pissed off. How can he leave me like this...WHY?

"I just feel like hitting something...beating it until I feel better." I look over to Mason who is hanging his head and staring at the floor as his mother continues with her rant. "...that when I wake up it takes all of my energy just to get out of bed."

She is visibly shaken by the words that came out of her own mouth. I can't help but reach up and touch her softly on the face. As she meets my eyes I give her a nod and a small smile, "Yes, that's exactly what I want you to tell me."

Silently, Michael enters the field house and stands near Emily. He reaches out and grabs Mason shoulder and to let him know everything will be ok.

"Hey sis, I'm going to take Mason with me, and go pick up Peyton from CJ's."

"No, that's ok. I think we're done here!" Anger is still in her voice. I'm just not sure who it is directed to...probably all of us. I didn't even get to say anything in rebuttal before Michael and Mason both shakes their heads to her.

"No Mom, you need to stay with Coach. Uncle Michael and I will see you at home in a little while."

"I feel like I'm being ganged up on."

"No Em, you're being cared for." She takes a deep breath and relents.

Michael and Mason leaves, and the air in the room suddenly becomes quite heavy. There was a lot more to say and do before we can move on.

"Now what?" Emily asks suddenly looking even more exhausted than before.

I reach out and touch her hand. Without a word I rub my thumb across her knuckles and pull her into a hug. She struggls against me for a few moments before giving into a small hug. I hold her stronger and pull her closer, and I can feel her muscles begin to let go a little bit more. After a few more minutes she finally gives up all resistance and sinks into my arms completely. She lets out a deep sigh, and I hold her even tighter. This is my sweet Em...my heartbroken sweet Em. She is hurting and I wish I could take it all away.

After a long while I pulled away from her enough to see her face. "I'm here for you. I'll be here for as long as you want me. You don't have to go through this alone anymore...I've got you." I pull her back into my arms letting her know I meant every word.

As she clings to me, I am surrounded by the soft clean smell that is uniquely Emily...a smell as soothing as soap and water with just a hint of vanilla. "I love you," I say as I place a kiss on he top of her head.

"I love you, too. Thank you..." Smiling, I bury my face in her neck, and engulf her in the biggest bear hug her tiny frame can handle. She giggles as I put her back down after swinging her around.

"Well, ok then," I say smiling. "Let's get you fixed."

"I'm broken?"

"Em, I don't know...you tell me."

"I guess I am broken."

"Well now that's established, what's first?"

"If I knew what to do, I would have already done it, and we wouldn't be having this conversation." Well, she's right about that.

"Ok, talk or hit? Pick one." She wrinkles up her eyebrows at me like she doesn't understand. "You said you wanted to beat something until you felt better. I have the something."

I walk her into the weight room where a punching bag hangs from the ceiling. "The boys use this for tackling, but you're going to punch. Let's wrap you up so you don't hurt yourself." I pull out the athletic tape and proceed to tape her hands. "You're not exactly dressed for this, but it'll do. Let's get your shoes off so she doesn't fall over in those heels." She is dressed in black slacks with a purple, gray, and white knit blouse that drapes loosely over her shoulders, and like always her high heel shoes.

Taking the position behind the bag, she throws the first punch. It's a bit weak because her try was weak.

"This is silly."

"Give it a try, like you mean it." The next punch is a bit more forceful. "Good, again." She hit the bag again, and again, and again.

"Talk to me Em. Why are you so mad?"

"Because he left me all alone to be mother and father to my boys."

"Ok, tell Patrick about it...don't hold back." And she didn't. For the next fifteen minutes or more, she lets him have it. With each hit she became louder and the hits became harder. Not once does she look like she was close to tears. She just looks angry. She is still holding too hard to too much. This is not an easy fix. This is going to take a while to break through all of her defenses and let her fall apart so she can move on.

She is sweaty as I reach for her hand and pull her into a hug to stop the abuse of the bag. She collapses in my arms. I hold her tight and kiss the top of her head and just stand strong for her to hold on to. She sinks into my arms as if her life depends on it...my sweet broken Emily.

"I'm sorry. I didn't mean to interrupt, but is everything ok?" Emily pulls away from at the sound of the voice, and we look to our intruder.

"Yes, everything is fine. Foster was just helping me with something."

"I could see that." Cooper glares at me and then back to Emily. His expression toward her is one of disappointment and contempt.

"I was picking up Chinese food for the girls and thought I would check on you, see if you wanted something to eat. I guess you have other plans."

"I was just about to follow Emily to her house to talk with Michael. Do you want to join us? You can bring the girls with you."

"I don't want to intrude on your evening."

"Nonsense. You're my friend, aren't you? Come on over eat with us, and we can all talk. If not you and Foster and probably Michael will talk behind my back anyway. You might as well be part of the 'Save Emily from Herself' campaign that they have going." I chuckle as she says her peace.

With some more encouragement on my part, Cooper agrees to join us, and we walk out together. I take Emily's hand in mine and give her knuckles a kiss. She smiles up at me.

Oh, my sweet Em.

Please vote.

Check out the picture of Michael and the video from Coldplay that was posted for this chapter.

Chapter 7 - The Inquisition

I f there is no struggle, there is no progress - Frederick Douglas

Chapter 7 - The Inquisition

Emily's POV:

Sitting in the driveway with my head in my hands, I ready myself for the inevitable. As much as I'm not looking forward to facing my brother and the conversation that is about to take place, I know it's needed at least for his peace of mind. Everything that has happened today has been out of love, I know that...but it doesn't make it easier to deal with.

I am physically and mentally exhausted from Foster, and the night is still young.

A knock on the window brings me back; Mason stands at my door hold Peyton. "You ok Mom?" Mason asked with more concern than a 13 almost 14 year old should have for a parent. He should be more carefree instead of worrying about me all the time. Honestly until a little while ago, I didn't even notice how much all of this is affecting him. I guess I should get my head out of my ass and start paying attention to my son.

"Yeah, I'm fine, just tired. Where's Michael?"

He's in the living room. He heard you pull up. He asked me to see what's taking so long." I smiled at him and looked at Peyton in his arms.

"What going on with you, Little Man? Are you playing Mason's shadow?" Peyton jumped out of Mason's arms and into mine.

"Untle My-Kill is here. He wants to play wit me."

"Oh, he does?"

"Yep - cars. He got cars." The way to my boys' heart...cars, blocks, or sport equipment. Michael always seems to know how to engage the boys. I take a moment to look at Mason and wonder what he and Michael have been talking about...at least he now has people he can talk to.

As soon as we reach the front door, Peyton announces in his 'not-so inside' voice, "Untle My-Kill, I'm back. Let's play cars now."

"Ok Peyton let me say hi to your mom first."

"Before we start, Foster and Cooper are on their way over. I need to go clean up a little and change out of these clothes so I am ready for the 'inquisition'." Michael smiles and kisses my forehead.

"We're just worried about you."

"I know. Let me change. I'll be right back."

Showering helped clear my thoughts for the moment. I tried to figure out exactly how I wanted this night to play out while I changed into yoga pants and a wine colored hoodie. I was definitely going for comfort. I scrubbed all remaining traces of make-up from my face and pulled my hair from its bun. I brushed my hair and tied it into a high ponytail before stepping out of my room.

I'm still sure how I wanted things happen, but I knew I didn't want to launch right in to their questions. I know Michael and Foster mean well, but I do feel a bit ganged up on. I haven't been sleeping, I've lost weight, and I feel like I'm about two steps behind in everything I should be doing. I do need help...I just didn't want to ask. Now I have to deal with the protection squad. I blow out a breath and head down the hallway to the kitchen.

Michael and Foster were in deep conversation as I entered the room. Both gave an attempt at a real smile, but it fell a bit short. Foster immediately took my hand in his and I could feel the warmth and his strength.

I feel like a high school girl all over again just being around Foster. I was never the giddy little girl with him...he was my wonderful solid friend. He was a rock...my rock. It was like I instantly felt better when he was around. He didn't allow me to feel weak because he gave me his strength. I couldn't feel sad because he would act like an idiot just to make me laugh. He always knew what I needed and he always gave it willingly.

Looking at Michael and then to Foster, "I won't answer any questions or begin this conversation before we sit down and eat. I don't think I can do this on an empty stomach." Both men chuckled and agreed this could wait.

Cooper entered the house with Addy and Chandler in tow. An assembly line of helpers brought plates, forks, chopsticks, and cups to the table. It was days like this I was thankful for my large dining table. Michael and Foster added the extra leaf and brought in two more chairs, and then we all sat down to eat.

The center of the table looked like a Chinese buffet. Even though our dinner conversation was kept light, the tension was still felt. Most of the talk centered on the three older children with their discussions of upcoming events, their school day, and their friends.

As soon as we finished our meal the assembly line brought the dirty dishes from the table to the kitchen. The dining room was put back the way it was found and the kitchen was cleaned. The children were excused to play on the Wii even though they preferred the playstation-the Wii was more active.

The kitchen was completely silent after the children left, and I didn't want to be the one to break it, because I wasn't going to give them more than what they were asking. I did not want to volunteer information, and I wasn't sure if they knew what to do first. So, we waited.

'Saved by the bell' well the doorbell. Michael went to answer and brought back CJ and homemade brownies.

"Hey sis, Keira wanted me to bring this over with me." Oh, now I get it. They were waiting for reinforcements.

"I see we waited for the Inquisitioner and Chief..."

"Ha, Ha, funny," CJ said.

I let out a deep breath and resigned myself to hear the men out. CJ began with how much they cared about me and were worried they were for me. I looked at the face of each of the men...Foster, Michael, CJ, and Cooper. Why was he here? I know he was invited to eat, but I figured he would leave the conversation became to heavy.

I barely know and here he was part of this group. I gave him a half smile and his gaze moved from my mouth to my eyes. They locked me. I can't 'not' look at him. I feel like he's trying to look into my thought and capture my soul. He just studies my face without expression. What is he thinking?

Foster's hand touches my shoulder then my neck and then he begins to rub up and down my back. He draws my attention away from Cooper and back to my brothers and him. He leans in and whispers, "I'm here for you, Sweets." He places a soft kiss on my temple and I lean into the kiss and close my eyes. This small gesture gives me the strength to talk.

"I know you guys are worried about me. I was just trying to learn how to do all of this by myself. I thought by now it would get easier, and I would have a pretty good routine. I guess I'm wrong."

"Why are you trying to do this by yourself? Don't you know you have us?" Michael wasn't too pleased. "I know you're independent, but damn girl, you're not alone."

Tears stung the back of my eyes...I am nothing but alone, I wanted to say. I could feel anger creeping up and burning through my body. Other than my family and Foster I have no one...they have their own lives and I can't ask them to give up their time for me. Foster must have felt the tension in my body. He leaned down again and whispered, "He's not mad. He's hurt." I felt his hand gently rubbing my back to help sooth me.

"Yes I am," I whispered to Michael.

"No Sis, you're lonely-not alone."

"Thank you for the clarification." I couldn't hide the sarcasm in my voice.

CJ shook his head at me. "What do you need from us to help you?"

"I need you to bring Patrick back." CJ flinched, Michael grunted and Foster pulled me back into his chest, and then buried his face into my neck. "You know we can't do that."

"I know, but they asked." Cooper looked at me like he didn't understand what was going on. I guess they haven't filled him in...well I'm not going to do it.

CJ shifted and asked that we all sit down. I chose to stand, because I felt the urge to bolt at any moment. Foster kept his position behind me with one hand on my back and the other holding my hand. I could feel his breath on my hair and it made me feel calm. Just like when I was a kid, he was always able to do that.

"How much sleep do you get?" Ok that was random, and coming from Cooper it was a little weird.

"I get enough."

"No, I mean in hours-how much?" He looked a little pissed. My brothers looked at him and then me waiting for an answer.

"I don't know a few."

"How much?"

"Two to four hours depending..."

"Depending?" Michael asked.

"Depending on the dreams." CJ closed his eyes.

"How long has this been going on?" Foster asked.

"It started before Christmas." I didn't tell them that I keep getting less and less sleep, or that sometimes I'm scared to fall asleep.

Just then Mason joined us. He asked Michael and CJ if he could stay. I was about to say no, but both of my brothers told him yes.

"Looks like the first thing that we need to do is help you get some sleep. I love you sis, but you're starting to look like shit." Foster chuckled and Michael smirked. Ha, ha, funny...

"Thank you very much," I said. I looked over at Cooper to see his reaction to my brother's jackass comment. He wasn't looking at me as if I looked like shit. In fact I had to catch my breath; no man looks at me like Cooper was doing. I immediately had to look away, his eyes were very intense and on the verge of making me uncomfortable. This was not a friendly look, it was something different...

Mason leaned in to whisper something to Michael and he nods his head. Our conversation turns to my need to visit a doctor and have a check-up. My brothers were worried about my lack of sleep and weight loss. They think I may need something to help me sleep until I can push through my vivid dreaming.

Even though I felt like I was under a microscope when it came to the men in my life, I knew they were just concerned. They weren't mad or blaming me; they were trying to support me in their own possessive alpha-male way.

I tried to look at this group as an outsider and it was quite humorous. Well, it was until..."Who have you been sneaking out to see?" With that every set of eyes in the room was on me.

"I beg your pardon?"

"Mason thinks you've been seeing someone." Michael asks, and Foster's head came around he gave me the most quizzical look.

"What are you talking about?" I looked straight at my son.

"Thanks a lot Uncle Michael. That was smooth." Mason cast his gaze toward me. "In the mornings, I know you leave the house really early. I've seen you, you look dressed for a run, but I've heard you talking to someone in the back yard sometimes...who is it?"

I was stunned. He thinks I am out with someone.

"She's with me," Cooper said as he stared straight at Foster. "About two weeks ago I saw her on the walking track early in the morning. It was still dark out and she was alone. This might be a good neighborhood, but it's still not completely safe. I knew you would worry about her, if you found out...so I told her from now on if she wanted to go for a run early in the morning to call me so she wouldn't have to go alone. I was just keeping her safe."

"Thanks man," Foster said.

Cooper looked over at Mason, "We cool?"

"Yea, thanks."

I rolled my eyes and leaned across the kitchen table toward Cooper. "You could have at least told them I brought mace with me and almost used on you the first time. You almost make me sound helpless...but thank you anyway." I gave him a quick wink, and he flashed a smile that almost stopped my heart.

Peyton came in the kitchen rubbing his eyes followed by Addy. "I think he's tired."

"He is sweetie. Boys, if you will excuse me. I have a little man to get to bed." I bolted out of the room before anyone could volunteer to take care of Peyton for me.

I did not hurry back. I took time to give Peyton a bath before changing him into his pajamas and reading him a story. As I placed him in his bed I heard someone in the doorway.

CJ was watching me with a small smile on his face. "Emily, you're doing an amazing job. I don't know how you do it all."

"I can't be doing that great of a job, or you wouldn't be here right now."

"No Sis, you're doing a great job at being a mom and dad to your kids, where you need help is taking care of YOU. That's why I'm here...that's why we are all here. YOU."

He leaned in and gave me a kiss on the forehead and engulfed my small body in a big ol' CJ bear hug. "Ok, let's finish this," I say as we head back down the hall toward the kitchen.

Mason was gone. probably playing games with the girls. Foster stood back up and took a place at my side. I leaned my head on his arm. Without my heels I am not quite as tall as his shoulder. He placed his hands on my neck and gently rubbed causing much of the stress to be released. "Thank you," I said as I looked up at his face. "Anytime."

"I can tell you guys are up to something...spill." I looked at all the guilty faces in the room.

"We were just coming up with plans to get you out of the house more. Not just for work..."

I let out a deep breath. "Oh, great! Now I'm a charity case."

CJ's face that was usually jovial became angry. "You are not now and never will be a charity case. Look around this room. These men want to see you happy, healthy, and independent. If the roles were reversed you would come to their aid. They get the opportunity to help you first."

"I'm sorry." I felt the burn of tears for the second time today...I do not cry! I wipe my eyes before the tears could escape. "Ok, so tell me. What's your plan to fix me?"

Foster gave a small chuckle and kissed my temple. "That's my girl."

"First off your social calendar has now been filled. I know you don't have many plans outside of work and soccer right now, but we all do and we are including you in our plans." Michael gestured to all the men in the room. "Before you begin to worry, most of it is family activities...your boys are included. Second, spring break is in a couple of weeks. Do you have plans?"

Just as Michael asked about spring break Mason and the girls entered the kitchen. "Yeah, Mom's taking me to some professional soccer games. Dad planned a family vacation for us before..."

I didn't let him finish. "We were going to go to some games. I haven't worked out the details since now I would have one less adult helping." I looked at Mason. "I need to work out some logistical problems. When these plans were made we expected to have two adults, so you wouldn't have to help with Peyton and you could enjoy the trip more."

I was about to explain that I was going to ask my parents to go with me when Michael interrupted. "Where are the games? If you're going to Dallas, I could go and help you."

"London and Barcelona."

"What?" CJ was a bit astonished by my travel plans.

"Patrick was expecting us to move to Arkansas in late March. He was taking three weeks off for moving and a vacation. The trip has already been paid for. Don't worry about it. I was going to ask mom or dad to go with me, because I'm not willing to leave Peyton behind for very long."

I quickly changed the subject to other people's plans. Chandler and Addy were going snow skiing with a youth group, CJ was taking his family to the beach. Cooper had just hired a new office manager and would be working during the break. Foster didn't talk much he just kept his hand on my back to remind me to stay strong.

Please vote or comment...I would like to know what you think.

Don't worry you'll find out what happened with Patrick soon enough, but Emily needs to be strong enough to tell you.

Please check out the video from Lifehouse and the picture of CJ that was posted for this chapter.

Chapter 8 - Making Plans

Walking with a friend in the dark is better than walking alone in the light.--Helen Keller

Chapter 8 - Making Plans

Cooper's POV:

For March it is bitter outside this morning. I know it's going to get up to 65 F outside, but why does the day begin below freezing? If it wasn't for Emily's text, I would still be curled up in my nice warm bed waiting for my alarm. I don't really want to go, but I could think of worst ways to begin my day.

I hurry out of the backdoor toward Emily's hoping she isn't already outside waiting for me. I know she has enough men in her life trying to protect her, but I'll gladly add myself to that list. At first I did it for Will, but now...

Rounding the corner toward the woods, I see Emily coming down the path. She's dressed for the frigid weather. Even though it's cold she still has her hair pulled up. At least today she has her ears protected with a fleece headband. Come to think of it, I don't think I've ever seen her hair down. Usually it's pinned up in a bun thingy, but last night she just had a ponytail.

Her hair is wavy and I just wanted to touch it. I doubt Will would have appreciated me doing that, because he really seems to like her.

Last night he couldn't keep his hands off of her. I'm happy for him. He finally has a girl I can at least tolerate. I'm not sure how serious this relationship really is but it didn't even faze him when she said she wanted her husband back. He seems to want to be with her no matter what.

"Good morning," I say as Emily joins me on the walking path. "What are you listening to?"

"Seabirds."

"Don't You Know You're Beautiful?" She nods, and I smile at the double meaning of my question.

"Yeah, you know that song?"

"I do," she puts in her ear bud and adjusts her music then gives me a smile that takes my breath. "It fits," I whisper.

She sets our pace in a slow jog. Her iPod is just loud enough to hear the tempo, but soft enough for us to talk.

"I'm sorry about last night. I can't believe you stayed for all of that." She looks a little embarrassed. She shouldn't be, it just shows how much she is cared for...and I was included in the group. I can't even begin to wipe the smile off of my face. I've only known her a short time, but I'm glad to have her around.

"I think you're stuck with me now. Between Addy and Will, we are connected."

"I think it's you that may be stuck, but thank you anyway."

We keep a comfortable pace around the track. After our first day, we have spent almost every morning running together. Only twice has it rained us out. Emily is building up to two laps. She could do it now, but not at a steady pace like she wants. Her pace just picked up. "What song is playing now?" I ask.

"Remember the Name."

"I don't think I know that one."

"It's one of Mason's warm up songs. He made this playlist for me the other day. This is the first day I used it. I chose the slower songs and he added the faster ones. He even put Wavin'Flag on here for me. He loves that song...it gets him mentally ready for a game." She pulls an ear bud out and hands it to me. I have to run close to her as I hold the bud to my ear. "Do you like it?"

"I can't tell. It sounds ok, but I'll have to listen to it later I think." She takes the ear bud and puts in back in her ear.

We continue with our run. After a while we slow down again. She must be back to the slower music. Dawn in finally breaking and I can see Emily better through the half light of morning. I've never envied my friend Will as much as I do this morning. He is one lucky man. Emily is absolutely beautiful inside and out. I keep looking over at her. I can definitely understand why Foster thinks he is in love with her...she is amazing. I heard him tell her he loves her. I wonder if she feels the same, or is she pining away for her husband that left her.

"About last night, it seems that everyone knows what happened with your husband." She stops dead in her tracks, and looks like someone just hit her in the gut. "I'm sorry. It's none of my business. I was just curious, and I don't need to know. I'm sorry."

"It's ok. I'm just not ready to talk about him...not yet, maybe not ever."

I nod my head toward her. "Come on let's finish this run." We cut through the middle of the field as we got past the half way mark. She finishes just over a lap and a half by the time we made it to her backyard.

"Would you like to come in? I can make you some coffee if you would like."

Spend more time with you, yes. "I would. Thank you." She moves into the kitchen and prepares coffee, but only enough for one person.

"You're not going to join me?"

"I don't drink coffee anymore. My body doesn't need the caffeine. I usually have decaffeinated Earl Grey tea. I'm sorry. I just assumed about the coffee. Would you prefer some tea instead?"

"No, thank you, coffee is fine." I look around her house. It's immaculate. Even better than it was last night, and that's when it dawns on me she's been a wake for a while-a long while.

"What time did you get up today?"

She averted her eyes. I know this is a sore subject, but I need to know.

"What time?" I ask again.

"Two."

"I see you didn't go back to sleep," as I gesture to her home.

"No, I couldn't."

"You want to talk about it?"

"No, not really. You could say that my dreams keep me from sleeping."

"Dreams or nightmare?"

With a half smile that did not even come close to reaching her eyes she said, "Dreams-they're a bit realistic." She spins herself around to gather the coffee and tea.

"How do you take it?"

"Cream no sugar." She brings mine in a disposable cup and lid.

"I wasn't sure how much longer you could stay. So, I hope you don't mind I made yours to go."

"Thank you. I only have a few minutes before I have to go wake up Addy for school."

"Mason will be down any..." She didn't finish her sentence because Mason was at the bottom of the stairs.

"Good morning, Mason," Emily greets him with a smile and a quick peck on the cheek. He kisses his mom on the forehead and greeted her. "Morning Mom. How was your run?"

"I'm at a lap and half." Mason nods his head. "That's good. You're getting closer to you're 10k."

"Morning," he says in my direction.

"Good morning, Mason. I've got to go. You guys have a great day." Just as I got to the back door, I see movement in the woods. For a moment I feel panic, thinking that Emily and her family would be unprotected, but then I saw what was moving. "Hey, come here...look at this."

In the woods not quite forty feet from the deck, is two fawns and a doe. Emily and Mason moves over near me and we spent a few minutes watching them until they moved farther into the woods.

I say goodbye again and go back to my house to get Addy.

To my surprise, when I turned off the house alarm, I find Addy coming down the stairs asking me if I just came from seeing Mrs. Cahill. When I gave her the answer she had a smile that matched how I was feeling.

Just before noon, I got a text.

Will: Karaoke Saturday@ Jo-Jo's...dinner at 6:00...yes or no

Me: Karaoke always a yes

Will: It's a surprise for Emily. Don't tell.

Me: Got it...plans tonight

Will: Dinner at 6:00

Me: What to bring?

Will: Wine and bread

Me: See you then

Emily's POV

I love Wednesdays. Not only is it half way through the work week, but that is my day with an extra plan period. I have some catch-up time. Today, I called the doctor and made an appointment for Friday afternoon, because my brothers would hound me until I did. I was already taking half of the day off to meet with the lawyers, so I might as well make the whole afternoon productive.

Mom was coming over at 11:30 so she could go the appointments with me. She knows I'm a big girl, but that doesn't keep her from worrying about her only daughter. She's really not going to get anything accomplished; she's just being my supportive mom.

When I talked with her earlier, I asked her about her plans during my spring break. I kept the conversation light, like I was just coming up with ideas for the boys. I knew she would drop her plans in a second to help me, but I didn't want her to do that. She and Dad were going to go to my Auntie Ella's house in Missouri for a few days to see their new great niece. This means I need to talk to Michael and see if he could go on an all expense paid trip to England and Spain with me. If not, I'll just make the best of it on my own with the boys.

Keira brought Peyton by the school just before the students were dismissed. Addy was super excited when Peyton wanted her to pick him up. She acted like the Queen Bee as she showed off Peyton the rest of the students. Peyton loved the attention from both my students and from his Addy. I was keeping Addy with me to drop off with Foster after practice. She took Peyton outside to the kindergarten playground for a few minutes as I gathered my materials and prepared for the next day of school.

The day had ended up very nice considering how cold the day had begun. My morning run with Cooper was not as awkward as I thought it would be. After last night I figured he would have pitied me more than he did. Or maybe he was just able to hide it really good either way...it was a nice morning.

I gathered up my belongings and the children and headed to the soccer field. I was able to watch the last 10 minutes of scrimmage with Mason in the goal. He was doing a good job of blocking the shots from what I could tell. One of the forwards was a very strong player. He had a good strong kick, and was able to think ahead before attempting a shot. Mason was able to block all of them, but he definitely had to work at it.

Even though his back was to me, I could almost see Foster's smile as he was sizing up his team. Only a couple of more days before the season's first game... against Greenbrier.

I walked up to Foster after the boys left the field. "You look like you're up to something. What gives?" I had to ask, because he had his 'Evil Foster Face' on. The face that in my childhood meant he had plans that would end with my utter embarrassment. I don't know what he is planning, but part of me can't wait to find out.

"Nothing, not a thing." Cue evil grin. "You ready for Friday?"

"First game of the season, you bet I am. I hope you want a big cheering section. We're playing against my cousin Kenny's youngest child. He's the Panther's number one striker. All my relatives within a 50 mile radius will be at the game cheering for both boys...not caring one bit about either school or team. My grandmother is thinking of it as a mini family reunion. God bless her."

"That's going to be great. Maybe I could let Coach White to take over the game and I could join you in the stands."

"I'm sure that would go over real well." I couldn't help but laugh at him...just the idea of him in the stands instead of on the field was comical.

"Your boy is doing a good job. I'm thinking of starting him in the goal." I can't believe it. Mason is going to be so happy. As of Monday, he was thinking Foster was going to start in as mid-field. He didn't want it, but he would have taken it. "I haven't told him, yet. I'm giving out positions tomorrow after our last scrimmage. Just to make sure."

"I'll keep it to myself. By the way, who was playing forward just now; the one with faux hawk?"

"That was Jac. He's good. He's got a great foot and good head. He may look like a star, but he plays with the team. That's rare at this age...at any age."

I chuckled. "I couldn't help but watch him, he shines on the field."

"It's easy talking to you about this. I know you're my friend and all, but sometimes parents have their own agenda. It makes it hard to talk to them about the team; you just seem to get it." I can't help but smile at my friend's compliment.

"Hey, you want to come over for dinner tonight?" Cue evil smile again. He batted his eyes at me and I couldn't help but laugh. "I made my mom's lasagna." My stomach growled my answer for me. "I take it that means, yes?"

"Yes." Just then Mason came barreling across the field being chased by Addy, and he scooped Peyton into his arms. I could hear the giggles from the team's bench.

"Let me get my son home and cleaned up. What time would you like to come over?"

"How about 6:00?"

"Sounds great...I'll see you then."

I guess it is true-my social calendar was going to be full for a while.

Cooper's POV:

I pull into Will's driveway and Emily's old dark grey Honda is there. I let out a breath, not because I don't want to see her, I'm just not in the mood to see Will's hands all over her again. Addy squeals as she leaves my vehicle, "Mrs. Cahill is here. Uncle Cooper aren't you happy, Mrs. Cahill is here. I like her."

"Yeah, I'm happy. You go run on inside. I need to grab some things from the back."

The smell of Ms. Alma's lasagna fills the air. Will has done a good job of learning how to make his mom's lasagna. It's really good but just not quite as good as his mom's. As I entered the kitchen I was met by the most beautiful set of blue eyes. Emily smiles and greeted me, but I couldn't stop looking at her eyes. For someone who survives on only a few hours of sleep a night, you couldn't tell by how her eyes dance and sparkle right now. Someone near me clears his throat and I find Will holding Peyton and studying my face.

"She has that effect on you, too? It's sometimes hard not to stare at her."

"Yea, sorry man...I guess she does." Emily looked at us both with a very confused expression. She has no idea how she affects others. I turn back to Will.

"You're a lucky man."

He winks at Emily and says, "She's my friend and I love her. So, yeah...I'm lucky." His smile is big and bright as he stared at her.

"Thank you, Foster. I love you, too." There was not a hint of teasing or sarcasm.

Will left with Peyton to go find some toys. Emily helped me empty my bags, and she made a salad before everyone gathered for dinner.

"Will, who stocked your kitchen? They did an amazing job. It doesn't look like a typical bachelor kitchen."

"Mom helped me set it up. I just maintain it. It helps that Chandler likes to cook, and understands how to keep a kitchen organized."

Emily focuses on Chandler. "What do you like to cook?"

"I would like to cook a lot of different things, but dad is a picky eater. So, I usually just make normal stuff like soup, spaghetti, chicken, or other easy stuff."

"What would you like to cook?

"I would have to think about that. There are too many choices running around my head. Chandler's face lit up with excitement just with the possibilities that await her.

Emily looked at the people at the table, and then back to Chandler. "If we have willing participants, we could cook up a nice feast. I like to cook, too; and you would get an opportunity to cook for someone other than your dad."

"That sounds great." Foster said and then looked at me and Addy, "How about it?"

"Awesome," Addy squealed before I could say anything.

"I guess you can count us in." I reach over and mess with Addy's hair.

"Come up with some ideas, we will make it happen. I could ask my sister-in-law Keira to join us. Maybe we could even get Addy in the kitchen." She waggles her eyebrows to Addy as she said the last part.

Addy immediately looked at me, "Could I, please?"

"Of course you can." I looked at Emily and smiled then mouthed 'thank you.' She sure knows how to make my niece feel like she is wanted. "As long as it's not a bother."

"Of course it's not. I can't wait to start...how about Sunday?"

Both of the girls pulled their fists back in a little cheers and said, "Yes."

Emily began telling us about living in California on what she called the international street. She described the houses and area to the point that I could actually see it through her eyes. Mason loved living in the desert. He said he was only a block away from the desert trails and used to bike a lot. He described climbing a hill not too far away from their house and it was high enough to watch fireworks from town on the Fourth of July. In fact, there were no trees, and you could actually see the fireworks from a neighboring town also. He said it wasn't very close, and not as fun to see, but you could still watch them.

Emily went on to say how she had many different countries represented on her street. Her neighbors to her right were from Vietnam, to her left were from Pakistan, across the street were from Peru, and at the corner her neighbors were from Greece. There was also a lady from Northern Ireland, a couple from Japan, and a sweet German family. She said it was because of all the military in the area and some of the specialized projects brought in people from other countries. She used to get together with the ladies from her street once a month and cook. She said it started as 'ladies night pot luck.' The food was so good that pot luck morphed into cooking lessons. They were sharing recipes and had little cooking lessons to learn how to cook the food. Some were easy, but others had complicated techniques. She said it wasn't hard, but more like multiple steps. She said she really missed that, and was looking forward to doing something like that on Sunday with the girls.

Listening to her talk, and watching how she made everyone feel so loved and cared for...I understood why Will loved her. How could anybody not love her? She was perfect.

"My kitchen 2:00 and dinner at 6:00." With that, talk of different favorite foods filled our conversation with everyone (including Peyton) giving suggestions. I watched Emily as she made plan with the kids. It's hard to keep my eyes off of her.

Will leaned over. "It's hard not to look at her." What? I need to stop looking at her. I can't tell if Will is mad or if he was he rubbing it in my face that she is with him? I just shook my head and watched the children talk.

As we finished dinner Mason asked, "Are you coming to the game Friday?" I looked at him and he had directed the question directly at me. I could tell by the way he was asking that he wanted me there. I damn sure was going to be there for him, and even his mom.

"Yeah, I was planning on it."

"Good, you can sit with my mom. My uncles and my grandparents are coming, too." I give him a smile as he talks to me.

"I bet there will be more than just those..."

He looked curiously at Emily and asked, "Who else will be there?"

"I'm not sure, but you have a cousin named Ethan that plays for Greenbri-ar. I'm guessing we'll have a lot of family show up for that game," she tells Mason. "He is my cousin's son...so 3rd cousin for you. Your grandma said he plays forward, so you should see him on the field no matter where Foster puts in during the game."

"Cool."

Our evening came to a close shortly after dinner. Chandler and Mason both had homework and a test to study for. I needed to get Addy home and ready for bed. She's going to need rest because our weekend just became very busy.

Please comment. Make suggestions or point out grammatical mistakes. I would love to hear from you.

Chapter 9 - Season Begins

F amily is not an important thing. It's everything. -- Michael J. Fox

Chapter 9 - Season Begins

Emily's POV:

My first official girls' night is tomorrow. It's Lil's birthday and she wants to go out and sing. I'm not much for karaoke but the idea of a night out with these girls sounds great. I'll be riding with Lil since she doesn't live that far from me, and she offered me a lift to Jo-Jo's. My boys are going to my parent's house after the game tonight and won't be home until Sunday afternoon. That's good- because I won't be in an empty house for long.

As I leave school mom is waiting in the parking lot. She didn't want me going to the lawyer without someone. She was worried that I might forget some important information. "I thought I was meeting you at the lawyer's office?"

"No, I don't like that you would be going by yourself. I came to give you a ride so you would not be alone. Is that ok?" she asked.

"Yes, it is. Thanks."

"Do you have any idea what's going to happen at this meeting?"

"No, I'm guessing that we will set a court date or something like that. They called this meeting. I didn't."

We drove in silence. It wasn't awkward but it was tense. I'm sure my mom doesn't know what to say to comfort me. I don't know if there is anything that can be said. This is not something she has any experience with. None of do.

My mom went into the meeting with me which is a good thing. I feel so numb, I'm sure I would miss what was being said. I am going to need her to help me remember everything.

My lawyer was recommended to me by a high school friend, Bill Jennings, that is a civil lawyer in the same law firm. Mr. Braswell is an older man that looks like he enjoys food. I've met with him twice so far. He is a no-nonsense type of man, but he has shown me great compassion.

He has us sit down and surprises me with information of a generous settlement offer. It wasn't so much the money as much as now there will be no court date; this case will be final, finished, over and done. My mother was overjoyed that there wouldn't be a battle, but I was just relieved that it was over. Then the lawyer said a few words that made my heart sink. "I had to offer you this settlement, but I don't think this offer is in your best interest."

"Why?" I'm not sure I was ready for the answer, but I couldn't take the words back.

"This is a no fault settlement, with the nondisclosure clause attached."

"I'll be damned. You have got to be kidding me? Is that why there is a settlement so early? I thought you said we probably wouldn't hear from them for at least 6 months."

It's been 5 months, 2 week, and 3 days since my life fell apart, and now I'm being told to shut up and takeit. Hell no! I tune out the rest of the meeting. My mom just holds my hand and continues to talk to my lawyer. I guess my mom was right, I was going to miss out on something important.

After a few signatures we left. I'm not even sure what I was signing, but my mom assured me this was what needed to be done. I know I did not accept the settlement, so I figure our next step will be court.

I took mom over to say hello to Bill before we left the office. My mom was happy to see him. He showed her pictures of his wife and his two kids. She gushed as most women do about baby pictures. Mom intervened when Bill asked about the case, but overall it was a nice quick visit.

After we left the lawyer's office my mom took me to the doctor. I think if I would have let her she would have gone into the room with me. Most of my visit was routine. They did draw blood for a few tests, mostly because the doctor thought I was anemic. He did prescribe sleeping pills. I have to take them for two weeks to help reset my body clock. He did suggest seeing a counselor instead of medication for what Foster and Michael think is depression. He would prescribe medication if and when he gets a report from the counselor. He did agree with Foster and my brothers to stay active and busy and to try and move on...easier said than done.

My mom stayed with me the rest of the day. She was meeting dad at the soccer game and Michael had volunteered to bring me home. I'm grateful, now I won't have to drive home from the game alone.

————

After an hour drive we make it to the stands to watch the last 15 minutes of the warm-up. Mason was looking good in the goal. He was blocking shots and practicing goal kicks. I look up into the stands and was completely astounded by the amount of family that was there. I haven't seen Cooper, but I save him a seat with us just in case he could come.

Peyton follows my mom to her seat. He was trying to take the steps without reaching up for the support rails. It was comical to watch so many people try to catch him each time he tries to steady himself as he climbs the steps.

My cousin Caleb shocked me by running up the stands and bear hugging me. "Yo, Em how's it goin'?" He asked with great enthusiasm, but did not give me time to answer. "Which one is yours?"

"Mason is warming up in the goal...number 1."

"Oh my god, he's huge. What do you feed him?"

Cooper comes up the steps and joins us and I introduce him to my family. He shakes hands with Caleb and you couldn't miss Caleb's once of over.

"Where are the girls?"

"They're coming, they stopped to use the restroom."

I motion to Cooper where I was going to sit, and he joined my parents in the stands. "Who is that guy? Better yet, who is he to you?"

He's a friend and a best friend to Foster. Speaking of Foster he's Mason's coach.

"Do you notice how he looks at you?"

"Who? Foster?"

"No, his friend." I quickly dropped that subject. I didn't need anyone to tell me that Cooper glares and me and usually looks upset in my presence.

I make my way up and down each of the rows to greet all of my family. We have about 40 people not counting kids; in all we take up the better part of six rows. Caleb and I make it to our seats and his dad gets up to give me a hug. He's deaf and signs to me, even though he does a good job with communicating with the hearing world, he always makes me practice my sign language. He won't even try to speak when he talks to me. Caleb tells him to be nice, because I'm old and out of practice. I tell Caleb to mind his own business. I haven't forgotten everything.

I reach my seat in front of my parents and Cooper and settle in beside Caleb. Addy and Chandler find some kids from school and sit with them. Caleb and I spend a few minutes catching up. He lives in Dallas now, but was coming up to see my grandmother because he had a four day weekend. He wasn't able to bring the kids because they had school, but he would bring them sometime in the summer.

My grandmother was right this was a bit like a family reunion. My cousin Kenny sat down the row from me, and told me not to get upset when he yells to take the goalie out. Ha, ha, very funny.

My grandmother and my Uncle Joe (Caleb's dad) sat in front of us. Uncle Joe had to turn around to sign questions to us, so eventually he ended up beside me. He said Caleb bothered him because he was too loud, Uncle Joe's running joke.

As the game got underway, I blocked out most of my family. The game was what I was here for, and I am one with the game. Not even five minutes into the first half, Mason had two big saves. He had multiple shots on goal that were easy for him to bat away, but two that were very scary from a mom's perspective. I know my kid cannot help win the game while he is the goalie, but he could lose it. I watch intently, and find myself the butt of a few jokes from my relatives about focusing so much I have no idea what's going on around me. A tornado could touch down and I wouldn't even know it. After the second time I heard something like that I took a moment to speak to other around me. Peyton had moved from my mom and dad to my brother CJ and Keira.

My grandmother commented on how handsome Foster was. Caleb didn't let that go unnoticed. "I wouldn't go that far Grandma. I'm far better looking than he is," Caleb told her.

"Yes dear, whatever you say." I snickered at her words, but then she looked directly at me. "He's single. So are you, and a good man like Will Foster won't be single forever."

"Grandma, we're not like that, we're just friends." I gave her the most serious look, but I doubt I got through to her. She has it in her head that Foster and I belong together.

I turned around toward my mother and found Cooper glaring at me. I swear sometimes he gives me the strangest looks. I decide to disarm him. It was almost half time. "Do you want to go with me to get a snack or drink? Peyton would probably want some popcorn."

Before he could answer, Peyton was in my lap wanting 'potcorn', or however he was saying that.

"I would like to, thank you." He gave me a sweet smile that almost took my breath away. Here I was think I was disarming him of his disdain for me...he was disarming me as well.

Caleb leans over and whispers, "I still don't like the way he looks at you." Well, neither do I, most of the time.

Peyton decides that Caleb's lap is more comfortable, because I keep jumping out of my seat to cheer. "Is this Gina's boy?" He asks as he is looking at Peyton.

"Yeah, he's great."

"If I didn't know better, he could pass as your biological kid."

"I know, he blends in to the family nicely."

"Have you heard from Gina?"

"No, not since her mom died. I didn't even see her when she signed over her rights, but it's for the best."

The buzzer signals half-time and I scoop up Peyton to go get popcorn. Cooper meets me at the steps and we walk together to the concession stand. "You look like you are enjoying the game," he said with a smile. "You're boy is a good player. He's not letting anything past him."

"I'm proud of him. He really wanted to play goalie which makes me nervous, but he seems to be really good at it."

Chandler and Addy find us hoping that we would get them a snack also.

We get our snacks and go back to our seats. Instead of sitting down from me by my parents, he takes the position directly behind me. I leave him there for a few minutes while I take Peyton around to see some of my relatives. Peyton high fives and fist bumps most of the men, and gets kissed from the women. He is enjoying his few minutes in the spot light before the second half begins. Peyton was settled beside Cooper and my dad and shared his popcorn.

Jac had scored three goals for our team so far, but right now the players were all down at our goal. I was nervous for my boy. He was attentive, but calm. His eyes were taking in all the players and watching the ball. I was amazed at how many shots were attempted and they were still coming. "That's six," Cooper reached down to whisper to me. "Six what?" "Six attempted shot, you're boy is doing fine. Enjoy the play." His words help calm me as I watched two more shots get batted away, and then he was able to grab the ball and kick well past half the field. I felt myself breath again. This was an exciting game.

At minutes left of the game I hear Kenny holler, "Now that's what I'm talking about...that's by boy." I am happy for my cousin, but sad for my son as Ethan makes the one and only goal for Greenbriar. I just hope Mason doesn't beat himself up for that. Final score us 4 Greenbriar 1.

After the game most of my family stayed in the stands to visit and wait for the boys. Michael was by my side to let me know he was taking my home. Even though I already knew that, I think he was just letting me know where he was when I was ready to leave. I wasn't ready to leave anytime soon. My family was loud and boisterous and a whole lot of fun to be around.

Foster came over after a little while and let us sign-out Mason so he would not have to ride the bus back home. He stayed long enough to greet my family and be congratulated on the game. "How was the game for you little Soccer Mom?"

"It was good. Very exciting...sometimes too exciting. Cooper had to calm me down once because I was so nervous for Mason." Foster tilted his head a little then looked at Cooper... "Is that so?"

"Yes that's so...your little girlfriend was a nervous wreck." Cooper told Foster and he smiled at his friend and then me.

Foster leaned over and whispered, "I need to see you later. Is that ok?" and I nodded my head.

He said his goodbyes and got on the bus with the team.

Mason came out of the field house as we made our way down to the track. I moved away from the crowd so I could congratulate him on his game. He had other ideas. He ran full force to me, bent down, and through me over his shoulders. I couldn't quit laughing. He paraded my around to my family with my rear up in the air...thank goodness none of my family took the opportunity to give me a spank. That would have been a little too much.

Cooper's POV:

Chandler and Addy ditched me as soon as we made it past the ticket counter. I had to listen to girl giggles and talk for the last hour. Usually, it is fun to listen to them, but today I feel I need a break. I can see Emily heading up the stair to the stands, and some guy picks her up and hugs her. Why does every guy have to touch her and hug her? Does this woman have no female friends?

As I reach her. She turns around to introduce me to her cousin. Cousin...I feel stupid. I look up into the stands and see a massive amount of people for a soccer game. Soccer in the south is not a big deal, football is a big deal. In the crowd I find Emily's parents and her grandmother, and then I see Michael, Keira, and CJ. I look over the faces in the crowd and it is easy to see that many of them favor. So, this is Emily's family.

She points to her parents and told me she would join me in a moment. I stand beside her. She is even tinier than I thought. I look down and notice she has on her running shoes. It's funny she wears them every day we run, but I never noticed how small she really was. This is also the first time I remember seeing her in jeans and a t-shirt. Granted the t-shirt says 'Soccer Mom' in sparkly letters, but still it's a t-shirt. She's always been either dressed up for work (over dressed for a teacher) or dressed for a work-out, this is casual Emily...this is cute. She still has her hair pulled up, this time in a braid that hangs over to the side so it doesn't interfere with her 'Cahill 1' on the back of her shirt. God, she's adorable.

I watch her as she makes the rounds to all of her family. This is the happiest I've ever seen her. She points out to the field finding Mason as makes his way to the bench waiting for the game to begin. She showed off her shirt when someone would comment on it, then she would spin around so they could see the back. She was a very proud soccer mom.

Before she was able to sit down she sinks into the chest of an older man that hugs her like his last breath depended on it. I've never seen her sink so deep into anyone's arms. His back is to me when she pulls back to look at the man, I swear she had tears in his eyes. She wiped her face and began making gestures to him, the man did the same in return, but not a word was spoken. She laughs and wipes her face again and continues with the gestures and then her cousin Caleb tells the man and signs that he should be nice to her. She's too old to remember all of that. She looks back and I catch her eyes and she waves and smiles at me.

When the game started it was fast paced and very entertaining, but not as entertaining as Emily. She was totally oblivious to others around her. She didn't yell much, but she would cheer some. She was mostly a nervous wreck every time the ball got close to our goal. During the second half, I'm going to sit a little closer to so I can remind her to calm down and enjoy the game.

Peyton was having fun moving from one lap to another. He was fun to watch as he pointed to his big brother and clap. After a while he ended in Emily's lap.

"Is this Gina's boy?"

"Yeah."

"He looks a lot like you."

"I know, weird huh? He fits our family though."

"What you and Patrick did...that's amazing. Not many people would have done that."

"Not really, but thanks anyway." Wait Peyton isn't her biological kid. I looked down at the boy and then to her. They look too much alike for him not to be hers. Wow.

At half time I went with Emily to get snacks. Addy and Chandler follow along hoping for their own snack. The girls decided to join us when we returned to the stands, and then their friends followed suit. I went and sat down behind where Emily had been sitting, while she took Peyton around to meet some relatives. He was getting high fives and fist bumps from every male and some of the women decided to kiss him. He didn't seem to mind any of the attention. This family was a very affectionate group of people, and Emily was at home right in the middle of all of it. Again, she looks to happy.

When she sat down in front of me, I heard her grandmother say, "Will Foster is a very handsome man. He's single and so are you. He's good, and men like him don't stay single very long."

"Grandma, we're not like that, we're just friends."

I hate feeling the way I do when I hear her talk about Will. I don't think it's jealousy, but I don't think Will deserves her. He's a good guy and all, but...

Peyton sits between Emily's father and me. He tries to share his popcorn, he's a cute kid. After a little while he finds the warm lap of his grandpa, but about ten minutes left of the game he leans over and says, "I want to hold you." I guess that is his way of saying he wants me to hold him. I look over at Jim and he nods his head at me to let me know it is ok. I hold out my arms for Peyton and he wraps himself around my neck and lays his head on my shoulder.

"He doesn't do that to just anyone. You must be special." Jim says.

All I can do is smile and hold on tight to this little boy that chose me to hold. Emily turned around to find Peyton, and her eyes glistened when she saw him in my arms. She put her hand on my knee and smiled at us. This was the first time she has ever touched me, and I can't describe the feeling that her touch has on me. Oh god, I sound like a girl. I just want more of her, but that's not going to happen...because she has Will.

Peyton fell asleep on my shoulders and I carried him out to Ms. Hannah's (Emily's mom) car. Mason carried his mom part of the way to the car, until she finally was able to wiggle out of his hold.

I know where this story is headed, but I would like some reader input to know if I'm on the right track.

Emily's soccer mom shirt and the song Wavin' Flags

Chapter 10 - Sing For Your Supper

My heart, which is so full to overflowing, has often been solaced and refreshed by music when sick and weary. - Martin Luther

Chapter 10 Sing for Your Supper

Emily's POV:

By the time the game was over last night the weather turned cold, but today was supposed to be nice and warm. I guess spring is finally arriving. I walk out on my deck to enjoy the early morning with a cup of earl grey tea. I miss coffee, but this is nice alternative. The house is quiet and I didn't have to worry about waking the boys with my noise. My mom took Peyton home in her car and my dad followed with Mason in the truck.

By the time Michael had gotten me home, Foster was sitting in the driveway waiting for us. I knew he wanted to come over, I just didn't expect him to be here first. Much to my surprise Michael didn't leave, he also wanted to stay and talk with me. I was starting to feel cornered again, and Michael must have sensed that because he immediately tried to put my mind at ease. It wasn't anything terrible; it's just that he couldn't go to London and

Barcelona with me for spring break. He had too many projects that needed looking after. He said if it was a shorter trip or closer to home he could have done some rearranging.

This wasn't news to Foster. Michael had already told him, and he was here to volunteer to accompany me and help with Peyton. I didn't like the idea very much, and it took some convincing from Michael that it would be ok. Michael let me know that this would be different if the person we were talking about was interested in me in a romantic way, but this was Foster we were talking about...he's like a brother.

"I know, but it doesn't look good."

"Don't worry how it looks. You know the truth about your relationship, so does Mason - no one else matters. It's no one's business but yours," Michael told me.

"Foster, how do you feel? Are you ok with this?"

"It was my idea. You won't enjoy the trip as much without help, and I want to go to Europe." He gave me a pleading look, like he was begging me to say yes. So I did.

When Patrick had set up this trip, his worry was comfort. So, instead of a being cramped in a hotel room for nine days, he had rented a three-bedroom furnished apartment just outside London, and a two-bedroom suite in Barcelona. Because of Patrick's preplanning, sleeping arrangements would not be an issue.

Foster and I talked about the trip. I showed him the itinerary. This was going to be his first trip outside of the Americas. He had been to Canada (which he barely considers another country), Mexico and Argentina. He was looking forward to crossing the Atlantic Ocean, and was excited that I said yes.

I told him about London and Barcelona. I took Mason to Barcelona when he was Peyton's age.

"And the last time I went to London, I came home pregnant."

"Not much of a chance of that happening this time," he smirked. Michael and I laughed at Foster's comment.

"If there was, you wouldn't be going." Michael stated matter-of-factly.

I was lost in thought when I heard a familiar voice. "I guess we're not running today." Cooper smiles at me as he makes his way to the deck and sits down. "I was surprised I didn't get a text or call this morning. I thought I would come check on you just in case."

"Sorry, Cooper. The boys are gone, so it didn't matter how loud I am this morning." I smiled at him and he returned it and I had to catch my breath. I composed myself and asked, "Would you like some coffee or something?"

"Only if you join me."

I raised my cup to him, "Actually, you would be joining me."

"Then, by all means...coffee."

"Would you stay for breakfast? I was about to make myself some eggs and sausage. Would you like some?"

"That sounds great." He followed me into the house and made himself useful by getting the food out of the refrigerator. As I made coffee and cooked, he kept me company at the kitchen island.

"Are you still going for a run?" I asked.

"You're the only reason I wake up early, and the only reason I run. So, if you're not going...neither am I." I am astonished by his words. He couldn't be serious. "I go to the gym about 3 times a week, but I only run with you."

"Oh," He only goes running because of me. He wakes up early because I want to run. He only wakes up early for me. Huh...

"Yeah...oh."

"You know you don't have to come with me. I could go alone, or I can find something else instead of running. You could sleep late."

"No, you will not go alone. Someone has to look out for your safety, even if you won't. Your running schedule helps me not be lazy, and to get up off my ass in the morning, plus I like spending some time with you without so many people around." He added the last part with a breath-taking smile. He has to know how that affects me, because he chuckled and shook his head.

Half past seven Cooper left to go wake up the girls. Chandler ended up spending the night with Addy, but Foster was picking up both girls so Cooper could go into work for a few hours.

The rest of the day was quiet and uneventful, but the evening held promises of a good time.

Lil arrived at 5:30. We were going to eat before the 'sangin' begins. I was looking forward to a girls' night even if it is karaoke. Robyn and Erica were meeting us at the restaurant. Lil says we would have a big crowd tonight. In fact, she didn't limit it to just women since she wanted to celebrate her achievement on making it another year. She says she wouldn't be surprised if more than 20 show up.

Lil paid for our dinner because she expected us to sing for our supper. Oh my god, I wasn't expecting to sing. I just wanted to hang out with my new friends. "Stop looking so panicked. We don't bite or 'boo' we only cheer." Lillian gave me a big smile hoping to ease my mind, but it didn't.

I never knew karaoke had ground rules, but with Lil it did. The last time they had gone out Hip-Hop was the genre of choice with Lil singing C-Lo. The mental image of a 60 year old cranking out F#@% You was hysterical. Tonight she wanted to sing some country. Much to my chagrin, I don't know very much country.... like almost none. Lil laughed and told me this was just karaoke so mess up and have fun.

As we were headed to the bar, I said, "You ladies need to drink A LOT! I sound better if you're drunk."

Lil laughed and Erica said, "Don't we all sister, don't we all?"

As we entered the club and made our way to a rowdy table, I noticed Foster, Cooper, Michael, CJ and Keira waiting for us. "Hi, Aunt Lil," Foster said and greeted my friend.

Lil smiles at me, "Did I forget tell you? This is Will's idea. He thought you needed a night out. It really is my birthday month, just not my birthday day...so technically this is your night."

I just shook my head at Foster and he feigned innocence. "I can't believe you." I looked at Lil and she just smirked at me. "Thank you, are you really his aunt?" I had to ask, Foster has about as many relatives as I do and I could never keep track of his family.

Foster interrupted, "No, but she likes me like family, so I call her Aunt Lil. Got a problem with it?"

"Nope, not at all." I just laughed at Foster and Lil. Erica and Robyn both hugged Foster. I looked around to all the people, and found Cooper watching me. He gave me a half smile as he studied Foster with the younger teachers.

I was introduced to the other people at the table. Two were teachers from Foster's school and their dates, another and his date was friends of with

Cooper, and then there was Lil's husband, and a few others I didn't quite catch. Everyone seemed to be nice enough, and as I put my purse down Michael hands me a Negra Modelo, and kissed my cheek. "You look good, tonight."

"Thanks," I respond, as I think 'I feel good tonight.' Lil told me to dress down a bit. I donned my black skinny jeans, royal blue long sleeved t-shirt, and a lacy asymmetrical vest. I'm dress more for fun than for show, but I'm glad Michael approves.

Lil explains her rules for the evening and everyone was happy with it. "Let's start this," Michael announced and motioned to CJ and Foster. This was going to be fun.

The guys got up to start the night. As the song began, I had no idea what it was. I don't normally listen to country, so I asked Erica. "Real Good Man," Cooper tells me. One of the lyrics is "I may be a real bad boy, but baby I'm a real good man." Suggestive much? Woah!

When the song finished Foster came to sit by me. "You need to get your 'flirt' on."

"I'm too out of practice for that." I haven't flirted with anyone other than my husband for more than 15 years.

Foster could see my reluctance as he pulled me closer to him and whispered in my ear. "Nonsense, pretend I'm Patrick and flirt with me. Find a flirty little song and let loose for a little while."

After a few more songs and a couple of beers, I felt a little bit brave. I picked up the songbook and began to look for any song I knew that could be considered country...I didn't want Lil mad. She made a point of saying "We are singing country...I don't care what any other table does." I look at Foster and think of Patrick and try to find a song.

"Ok, I found one. What do I do now?"

"You go give the DJ your name and song title and wait for your turn." After I did that I went outside and pulled up the song on Youtube so I could at least hear it once before I try and sing.

When I came back in Lil and the younger teachers were sing Pantoon by Little Big Town, or at least that's what Keira told me it was. Then it was my turn.

Foster squeezed my hand and wished me luck. As the music started I moved over to our table and sang to Foster like he was Patrick. When I Think about Angels by Jamie O'Neal

Why does the color of my coffee match your eyes ....Why do I see you when I stranger passes by ...,I swear I hear you in the whisper of the wind ...,I feel you when the sun is dancin' on my skin ....And when it's raining ....You won't find me complainin' cause

I made sure any touch I gave Foster was flirty, but definitely in the 'friend zone' not like what I would have done if it truly were Patrick.

When I think about rain...I think about singing --When I think about singing...its a heavenly tune --When I think about Heaven then...I think about angels --When I think about Angels...I think about you

Everything I do or think leads me back to Patrick, this is true. Foster is playing along with me as I sing; he is most definitely fun to flirt with.

The taste of sugar sure reminds me of your kiss ....I like the way that they both linger on my lips ....Kisses remind me of a field of butterflies ....Must be the way my heart is fluttering inside ....Beautiful distraction ....You make every thought a chain reaction

I catch Cooper's eyes and sing the rest of the song in his direction, because he is my friend and feel safe flirting with him, also. He takes it well, and plays along like Foster had done. I would have included more people, but that would have meant flirting with my brother YUCK!!! Or strangers and I'm not ready for that.

"Oh my god, that was amazing." Foster picked me up and spun me around. "Patrick was a lucky man," he whispered in my ears. I felt the tears prick in the back of my eyes.

I let out a big breath trying to compose myself, so I wouldn't cry. "I miss him, so much." He kissed me very softly on the temple and placed his forehead to mine and said, "I know, my sweet Em, I know." I wipe my eyes and sat back down and listened to a few more songs, then I heard Foster's name called.

Foster had announced that he had the perfect love song that truly expressed how he feels when he is with me, and then he laughs. "Really?" I couldn't wait to hear what song he chose even though I know Foster is going to embarrass me, because he never gets embarrassed himself. The boy has no shame.

Every time you take a sip ....In this smoky atmosphere ....You press that bottle to your lips ....And I wish I was your beer ....In the small there of your back ....Your jeans are playing peekaboo ....I'd like to see the other half of your butterfly tattoo.

The song sounds serious like a love song would, but the words are not. Almost everyone at the table is either watching me for my reaction or Foster, laughing. "What is this song?" I asked Cooper. "Ticks" was all he said in response and then chuckles. I shrugged my shoulders, because I have never heard the song before today.

Hey that gives me an idea ....Let's get out of this bar ....Drive out into the country ....And find a place to park.

Foster comes over to me, and rubs his hand down my face and smiles so sweetly. I'm still trying to figure out what he is doing.

'Cause I'd like to see you out in the moonlight ....I'd like to kiss you way back in the sticks ....I'd like to walk you through a field of wildflowers ....And I'd like to check you for ticks.

Ok, I knew he was up to something, but that is hilarious. I laugh so hard I could barely breathe. Cooper pats my back, "You've never heard this song before?" I tell him no, and continue laughing. After the chorus Foster takes his 'flirt' to other unsuspecting ladies. He was very entertaining to watch.

The song has a key change and Foster is back in front of me keeping eye contact and flirting.

You know every guy in here tonight ....Would like to take you home ....But I've got way more class than them ....Babe that ain't what I want.

When he was finished someone from another table started singing Single Ladies and a lot of women went up near the stage to dance. Keira and Robyn wouldn't let me sit this out and were pulling me up with them. Michael stopped them and I was thankful for a moment. Then, he reached down to my hand, pulled off my wedding rings, and put them on my necklace. "You're single now, have fun."

"Ok." Cooper watched me as I joined the group and Foster was cheering me on.

Cooper's name was called next, and he looked at me and then Foster. "I'll show you a love song - and up beat love song, but still a love song."

As the song begins Cooper puts his hand out for me to take. This is the first time I have ever held his hand. He is my friend, but not that kind of friend. Foster sees my hesitation and places my hand in Cooper's. He whispers, "Go have fun." I smile and let Cooper lead me to a stool. He's going to serenade me? Are you kidding? I'm part curious and part terrified, but still I still go. He smiled at me and said, "Last one Standing it's by Emerson Drive." I didn't know the song, but I wanted to hear him sing.

Queen of the night .... Life of the party .... It's all an illusion ... You can't hide that big of heartache .... So stop the delusion .... Waitin' for someone's rescue .... My arms are right here for you

Cooper opens his arms and has a complete sincere look on his face. He smiles at me and I have to catch my breath. It was a wonderful song and his voice was rich and deep. It's funny how some songs connect, but this one found a home in my soul. I felt the sting of tears and I gave him a weak smile and turned away.

Through the wind and the rain .... Through the laughter and pain .... Count on me .... And when life isn't fair .... And there's nobody there, I will be .... In a world of pretenders .... I am your defender .... I'll never surrender .... And when it all comes down .... I'll be the last one standing

I couldn't watch him as his song rips though me. I am no longer smiling I'm too stunned. Even this song doesn't speak of love, he was right...this is a love song. This song is a promise. As I listen to more of the song, I remember that he is just showing Foster what a love song is supposed to be like. I plaster a not exactly fake smile on my face and enjoy being in the spotlight for a moment. When he finishes the song he reaches up and caresses my cheek. My body reacts to his touch, and I loose my smile again. Breathe...breathe...breathe.

Music usually affects me, but tonight my emotions are all over the place. Robyn, Erica, and Keira sang Gun Powder and Lead, and were a little scary.

I would not want these women mad. Lil being the Lil decided to sing I Ain't Your Mama, which is a very suggestive song, and down right funny coming from her mouth. She must have been practicing that song, because she had moves to go with the lyrics. Foster graciously volunteered himself as her focus while she sang her song. Her husband just shook his head and said, "I can't take that lady anywhere."

I watched Keira and CJ tell each other secrets as lovers do. They were cute and I was lost in what they were doing when a song began. The song wasn't country, so it must be someone from another table. Cooper got my attention and asked if I was having fun. I let him know I was having a great time, and that I was happy he was here. The song is slow and and tells a story I almost missed the first line of the song, but then my heart stopped when...

She's sitting at the table, the hours get later ....He was supposed to be here ....She's sure he would have called ....She waits a little longer, there's no one in the driveway ....No one's said they've seen him

Oh my god...breath in, breath out, breath in...two big hands reach me and I hear, "Sweetie, it's time to go. Emily, look at me baby. Let me get you out of here."

Why, is something wrong? .... She looks back to the window

The song plays on, but my head is in a fog and my body wouldn't move. Foster wraps his arm around me and practically carries me outside.

Foster's POV:

"Oh shit," I get to Emily as quick as I could without causing a scene. She looks like she just hit in the gut. Her face looses all color, and I think she is about to faint. Oh my god, I've got to get her out of here. I use a calm voice even though I feel anything but calm. "Sweetie, it's time to go. Emily, look at me baby. Let me get you out of here." I help her to her feet and try to get her out without too many people knowing something is wrong.

Michael and Cooper join us outside. "I've got her. We'll take her home." Motioning toward Cooper, "Go say goodbye for us." I could see Michael is agitated. "It'll be ok. I'll take care of her. I'll call you if I need help."

"Ok, but that's my sister I am trusting you with."

"I know, man. I've got this."

He walks inside as Lil comes out with Emily's purse. She has to make sure Em was ok. That's just like her. Taking care of everyone.

"Is she alright?"

"She'll be fine. I think she just needed some air." She knows that's a lie, but that is what she will tell everyone else. She hands Emily's purse to Cooper, before she heads back in the club. Emily is light as I carry her to Cooper's BMW, and I scoot her over and pull her into my lap. She buries her head into my neck...but doesn't cry.

Cooper asks, "Is she ok?"

"I think so. If not, she will be."

Cooper's POV:

Emily clings to Foster as if her life depends on it. I was talking with her, and she was telling me how much fun she was having. She even told me she was glad I was there. I watched her pale just before Foster got to her and pulled her outside. I don't know what he saw or what he knows, but he didn't hesitate to take care of her even if he spent the whole evening flirting with almost every woman at our table. Emily needed him and he dropped everything for her.

As we got to her house, she turns to me and asks, "Do you want to come in? I think I owe you an explanation. I know Foster wants me to talk, and I wouldn't mind if you hear. I want you to know why Foster acts like I'm made of glass." She says the last part with a little chuckle.

Foster laughed and kissed her on the forehead. "I don't think you're made of glass, and I don't like you broken."

I would like to hear from you. I feel I'm writing in the dark, and I need you to be my light. Like or comment...let me know how I'm doing...this is a bit scary for me.

Foster's karaoke song has been posted for this chapter.

Chapter 11 - Reliving the Day

A happy marriage is a long conversation, which always seems too short - Andre Maurois

Chapter 11 -Reliving the Day

Cooper's POV:

We all sat in the living room in silence for a while. Will and I are waiting for Emily to talk. I guess she is trying to figure out how to begin.

"Do you know there are some days you never want to relive, but they are usually the ones your brain never lets you forget? September 30th was the last time I slept for more that 5 hours in a row. Patrick promised when I woke up on October 1st that he would let me sleep late that coming Saturday. It wasn't that I was really tired; I just wanted to sleep in. That never happened." I'm not sure where this story is going, but I assume she is going to tell us how her husband left her.

Will holds her hand and pulls her into his arms. He kisses her hair and mumbles something in her ear. "I'm sorry Copper. I'm not usually such a drama queen, but when it comes to Patrick nothing is easy."

"Don't worry about it, Em. Just tell us. Let it out. Is this the first time you talked about that day?" Will asks. She nods her head. He looks at me trying to figure out if I am ok with this, and I am.

"You know about two years before we adopted Peyton, I almost hated Patrick?" So, Peyton is adopted. "I had lost a baby, it was the second time, and it hurt like hell. Patrick and I grieved together after the first miscarriage. I was only 8 weeks along, we had barely found out I was pregnant before I lost the baby. It just wasn't meant to be, and I did come to terms with that. The second time I made it to 14 weeks and had already met with a doctor and began planning for a new baby in the house. When I lost it, I was devastated and Patrick didn't know how to comfort me so he didn't. I resented him, and then that resentment started turning to hate. We pretty much lived separate lives and for almost a month I didn't talk to him. He called my dad to come out to California. I figured he was calling an intervention, somewhat like you guys did." She gives me a small smile and she nestles her back closer into Will's chest.

"Patrick had another idea. He had asked my dad to stay with Mason while he took me to Hawaii for a week. He told me I needed a change of scenery, and he got me away from the house, where I wouldn't be reminded about the loss of my child. He spent time showing me how much he loved me, and how hard loosing the baby was for him. It was the first time we really talked about the baby. I had no idea what he was going through, because it hurt him too much to talk. He was patient with me. He told me if a week wasn't long enough, then we could stay longer. It wasn't long enough.

"By the end of the week, I fell in love with my husband again and I wasn't ready to go back to the real world, so we stayed a few more days. After that trip we were like newlyweds. I didn't think I could have loved him anymore than I did...that was until we got Peyton. Then, I found I could. You know, there not many things sexier than a handsome man holding a sleeping baby.

"He was my entire life. We made a pact that we would never start the day without connecting with each other, and that included the days when he had to get up too stinking early." She smiles to herself.

"He would hold me every morning. I take that back, sometimes I would hold him. Some days it was just a nice cuddle, some days it was playful and sweet. Some days he would even reset the alarm so we got up early and he would make love to me. Oh god, the things he could do to my body..." She blushes as she spoke. She is so adorable. Why would anyone leave her?

"On October 1st he was supposed to work late to sign off some projects he had been working on. He had less than 5 months before he would have a permanent change of station which is military talk for moving. We were supposed to take most of March as vacation and moving here. As you can tell I got here early and without him." Her eyes begin to water, but the tears don't come. She straightens her shoulders and adjusted her focus. I've never seen a woman so determined not to cry. "He called me that afternoon and told me he wouldn't be as late as he first thought. His first meetings finished quickly and he expected the last one to do the same. I was happy because Mason had algebra homework and I wasn't looking forward to being the helper." She smiles at me, I guess to make herself feel better. I've never wanted to hug anyone more in my entire life. I know what she is about to say must be painful, but she is doing everything in her power to say it without tears.

"He didn't come home by dinner, which was what I was expecting, so I called him. No answer. We had spaghetti, and Peyton was a disgusting mess." She chuckles and shakes her head, and for the first time since she started talking she looks me in the eyes. I saw nothing but pain. "I called him after Peyton's bath and Mason's homework, each time no answer." She takes a deep breath but shows no emotion. She stares at the wall without a word. Will and I just wait.

"Sweetie, it's ok. You can tell us. It's only memories." She sinks even deeper into Will's arms and he tightens his grip on her.

"At 10:07 someone knocked on my door. It was very late to have company, so I figured Patrick didn't have his keys out and knocked so I would open the it for him. I was laughing by the time I got to the door, because I was going to give him a little grief for not digging out his keys." Her eyes fill with tears, but she stops them again. When she lets go...

I just want to hold her and take away the pain, but I guess that's Will's job. "But it wasn't Patrick it was his friend Garrett Breda." She takes a deep breath.

"You don't have to finish if you don't want to. I know this is hard." Will says as he rubs Emily's arms and plays with her fingers. She watches his hands for a minute and says, "I'm ok, I need to say this. I need to get it out."

She looks at me and smiles so big that I almost believe that it was real. "As a military wife there is only one thing you dread. It's not that you're moving, or that husband is going off on a temporary duty, or that he is going to war...it's the visit." One single tear falls and she wipes it before others could follow. "I got that visit." I don't understand what that meant.

"Colonel Breda wasn't there to see Patrick he wanted to see me." Nothing, just silence for more than a minute. "He wasn't alone." More silence. Will begins to touch her hands again. "Garrett brought with him the base commander and the chaplain, and it was an official visit." She takes a deep breath and blows it out. Her chin quiveres a bit, but no tears.

"You know nothing good comes from an unannounced visit from a chaplain in uniform. Garrett hugged me and told me to hold his hand, and then he walked me to the couch in the living room. I told them I didn't understand why they were here, even though there could only be one reason. All three men were in dress blues, which was unusual. Garrett usually wore a flight suit or BDUs like Patrick did. I didn't want them in my house.

"Before they even spoke I knew what they were going to say; I just didn't know the details. The base commander began with 'I'm sorry to inform you' as Garrett squeezed my hand and sort of choked back his emotions. 'Col. Patrick Cahill was killed today in a collision as he was leaving work. It is still under investigation, but it appears the vehicle that hit Col. Cahill was traveling at a high rate of speed, and there were no signs that the driver attempted to break before the collision. Col. Cahill died of his injuries before the paramedics arrived.'

"I know the base commander was just trying to stay professional while he relayed the news, but it pissed me off that he had to be so dry...like he didn't have a heart. It was nothing like the man that played golf with my husband once sometimes twice a month for the last 18 months." I wipe away my tears and see Will do the same, but Emily is determined not to shed a tear. Maybe she is all cried out, but I don't think so.

"When? was the only thing I asked."

"They told me it happened less than an hour ago. I didn't believe them because Patrick was supposed to be home in time for supper. Garrett told me that his last meeting went longer than expected. He assured me that it really was him."

What do you say to that? There are no words. I misjudged her. I've never seen a woman as strong as Emily. Now I understand why she still wears her rings, and why Michael keeps noticing them. He's ready for her to move on with her life, but clearly this poor girl is still in mourning. Shit it hasn't even been 6 months; there is no way she is ready to move on. And there's my friend being her friend. I physically hurt for her. I wish I could take the pain away.

After a few minutes of silence letting the entire story sink in, Will asks Emily, "So, tell me what happened earlier? What happened at Jo-Jo's?"

"Nothing really, it's kind of stupid."

"Tell me anyway." She moves away from him enough for her to look at him.

"It was a song. Stupid, right? And I really hate that song."

"What song?"

"Almost a week after Patrick died, I still was crying nonstop. I think I was scaring the shit out of Mason. He was doing everything he could to get my mind off of Patrick's death." She takes a deep breath and blows it out. "I know it is understandable to grieve for a lot longer, but for the 13 year old boy who still needed his mom...I needed to stop. I got better, but I still cried a lot just not as much. I didn't go back to work since I knew I would be moving by Christmas. I started cleaning out the house of all the unwanted things. I was buried deep in the attic cleaning and sorting with the radio blasting.

"I was feeling better, because I had something else to focus on, and then that damned song came on and I couldn't get to the radio fast enough to turn it off." She looks mad as hell. If what she was saying wasn't so tragic, I would have laughed, because she is cute. "The song isn't much more than a story set to music. Not a good candidate for karaoke, but someone must have thought so. It's called 'Forever and Always'. I think it's by Parachute. It was the first time I had heard it, but I knew before the chorus that I needed it turned off. Needless to say I wasn't able to get to the radio soon enough. I heard the whole song.

"It tells a story of a girl who is waiting for her fiancé to come home, but he doesn't. She gets a call that he was in an accident and she needs to come to hospital. The story doesn't mirror what happened to me, if that is what you're thinking. It was that in the story, she got to say goodbye. That was the part that hurts. I didn't say goodbye. That song is a reminder that I didn't get to say goodbye to Patrick." One lone tear falls down her face and Will wipes it off of her cheek. He pulls her back in his arms and kisses her forehead and begins whispering to her again. I feel tears sting my eyes, and I look away to compose myself.

Will being the man to lighten a tense moment says, "Emily, if you were a dude, I would tell you to go get laid...but you're not. So, let's get you drunk."

BDU: is a military acronym for 'battle dress uniform.' It's kind of like fatigues.

Without a doubt I love both of these men, but for two very different reasons.

Please vote or comment. It took my almost a whole box of tissue to put this chapter on paper. I would like to hear from you.

I did not add the video of Forever and Always, but I did add a wonderful song by Ben Rector instead.

Chapter 12 - The Morning After

Chapter 12 - The Morning After

Emily POV:

Patrick walked out on the balcony and sat down beside me.

"It's nice to be away for home for a while, isn't it?"

"Hmmm." Was all I could reply because I didn't want to be anywhere near him. Part of me wanted to cling to him with all that I have, but the other part of me remembers I've suffered the loss of my child alone.

"This trip is for us. We need it." I look at him but say nothing. "Emily, I miss you. I know you are hurting, but you are not alone. I need you to know I am hurting, too." He didn't say anything more for a long time; he just stared out into the ocean.

"I think I fell in love with you the day we met. You are the most beautiful woman I have ever known, but it wasn't love at first sight." He took a deep breath then glanced at me. "It was when I heard you talk to your grandmother and brothers and Will that I began to fall in love." He smiled at me, but I didn't have it in me to return the gesture.

"I still remember the day we met. You and your brothers decided to surprise your grandmother for her birthday. You showed up for church and sat with her. She was so happy. I could see it on her face. You were only a row in front of me. I watched you that morning; I couldn't wait for service to be over so Ms. Esther could introduce me to you." I remembered that day too. I couldn't believe such as man as Patrick would want to talk with me. He stayed by my side all day.

"I was invited to eat lunch with you and your family, which I am forever grateful. It gave me a chance to talk to you and find that you even more beautiful inside. By the end of the day I was making plans for spending the rest of my life with you. I would say that was the best day of my life, but it was only the beginning. I have loved you since the day we met, and my love is still growing." He looked at me then raised his hand to caress my cheek. I was reluctant, but I allowed him his touch.

"Sweet Pea, I love you. I've missed you." He placed a sweet lingering kiss on my temple. "I know we have a lot of things to work out, but I want to do this together." He held out his hand to me. I took it.

We sat in silence watching the ocean. This was him reaching out to me, and this was the first step.

"I've missed you, too." I said without looking at him, showing that I was willing to take a step also.

Waking up my head hurts, my mouth feels pasty, and my body aches. I reach up to adjust my pillow, not wanting to get up quite yet, and my hands fall on a very hard, very naked chest.

I jerk myself up to find Foster curled up in my bed. My movement startles him, and he rouses. "How did you sleep?" he asks as if he belongs in my bed.

I am too stunned to speak. I just stare at him.

"Are you ok?" he asks. He reaches up and pulls my head down and kisses my forehead. "Do you have a headache?"

I just shake my head, and gather my hoodie. I leave him in my bed to sleep, while I go to the kitchen to make tea.

I sit on the deck with my tea watching the sunrise. The thought of last night's events are shaken off for now, and my dream about Patrick in Hawaii floods my mind. I trace the story from the beginning to the end and find joy in my memories for the first time in months.

Cooper comes through the woods to my backyard, wondering if I was going to run today.

"No, I think my hangover would not allow it."

"Sorry. How do you feel?"

"Confused, but fine." He is glad and is quiet for a few minutes. Confused was an understatement for how I feel. Foster was true with his assertion, he got me drunk. I pretty much put everything on the table. No topic was taboo last night. If it was asked, I answered it. I know that sometime after midnight, Cooper left, leaving Foster to take care of poor drunk Emily. I'm not sure how exactly Foster ended up in my bed, but he has a lot of explaining to do.

"Thank you." Cooper says drawing my mind out of my thoughts. He says it with such a sincere look, but for the life of me, I don't know why he is saying thank you.

"You're thanking me? For what?"

"For letting me stay. For opening up and letting me in. I'm sorry about your husband. And, I need to apologize to you."

"Why? What did you do?"

"I misjudged you. I thought you were cheating on your husband with Will. I wish you would have told me about Patrick earlier." I guess that was the reason for all of the strange looks he has been giving me.

"I wasn't ready to talk about him. I'm still not, but I'm getting there." I smile at him to put him at ease. "By the way, apology accepted."

"I'm not a very good hostess today. Would you like some coffee?"

"Yes, please." He follows me into the kitchen keeping me company as the coffee brews.

"Are you all set for today? Addy is excited about cooking lessons."

"I think so. As soon as I go over the menu with the girls, we'll head out for groceries. It should be fun." He looks skeptical. "Really. These are skills these girls will need to live on their own."

"Uuuuhhhh! Don't say that. I'm just getting used to having Addy with me, I'm not ready for her to move away and live on her own." I just laugh and shake my head...spoken like a dad.

Cooper and I spend better part of an hour on the deck. Since I shared so much of my life story with him last night, I decided to turn the tables on him. We started talking about his sister (Sydney) and her illness. He had just moved here to open the Mills Lumber (his third store) when she was diagnosed with ovarian cancer. By the time it was discovered it was stage 4, and she fought for 18 months until the disease took her from Addy and him. He was granted full custody of Addy, after he proved that he was willing to take on the responsibilty of raising a child on his own. His face softened a lot when he talked about how Addy and Sydney were so similar. He says it's like getting a pint sized version of his sister back.

Then, he began talking about his ex-girlfriend Charlotte. His expression did not lend itself to pain as much as disgust, when it came to talking about her. They had been together for almost two years. When he moved here, they tried to make it work by seeing each other every other weekend. After his sister died, Charlotte decided that was a good time to tell him she never saw herself as a mother, and did not think it was wise to continue with their relationship since there was a child. What a selfish bitch. She had told him that she couldn't see a future with him. He just shook his head and said, "Come to find out, she had been seeing someone for the last 4 months before she decided to break it off."

Coopers stomach grumbles and I offer him breakfast. He helps me with pancakes as I make eggs and sausage. As the first pancakes are coming off the grill, Foster opens the door to my bedroom. Cooper shot me a questioning look and I shrug my shoulders. "That smells great," he says as he greets me with a kiss on the head and says hello to Cooper. The ease of conversation that Cooper and I enjoyed has ended. Cooper stares at me as if he couldn't be in the same room. Shortly after breakfast he leaves and Foster and I have a chance to talk about last night.

Foster and I sat down to talk about the events of last night in the same place that began it all hours earlier.

After he had offered to get me drunk, I changed into something much more comfortable: yoga pants, tank top, and hoodie. All three of us sat in the living room talking and drinking. I had told stories of places I've been and lived, how much Patrick was missed in my life, and the plans I have for my boys. After four glasses of wine on top of the three bottles of beer from the earlier, I was sent to bed and Cooper left (he obviously didn't drink much). Foster stayed in the guest room because they thought I was too tipsy to be home alone. That did not explain how he ended up in my bed.

"Do you have many nightmares?" He asks. Totally changing the subject from where I was headed.

"Dreams and nightmares...but mostly very realistic dreams. Why?"

"About an hour after you went to bed, you started yelling in your sleep. It wasn't exactly screaming, but it was upsetting you. That's why I was on your bed. When you kind of woke up, I asked if you needed me to hold you. You said yes, and I fell asleep."

"Foster, you know how much it freaked me out to have you half naked in my bed?"

"Well, technically I wasn't in your bed. I was on your bed. Big difference. And by the way, next time, I'm stealing the blankets."

I just laugh and shake my head, telling him there won't be a next time.

Just before 2:00 Mason comes running in the house followed by Peyton. Mason has to show me what my father had gotten him for his birthday. -- a new mandolin. Peyton couldn't be out done; he has to show me his toy guitar and his soccer ball. Both boys will be celebrating their birthday during spring break. My parents come in and listen to my boys tell me about their weekend adventure. As soon as Mason finishes with what he wants to share, he heads off to his room.

Since Chandler had chosen the menu for the evening, my mom and I set up the kitchen for cooking class. By 2:00 everyone was here and our real work began. We ended up with five cooks in my kitchen, and all of the men in the backyard. While we were shopping, prepping, and cooking, the men set up the net for the soccer goal and marked out the boundaries. Peyton kept going from Foster to Cooper to get carried around, but he made my dad sit to hold him. Mason and my nephews were playing by the time dinner was ready.

Chandler and Addy plays hostesses for our meal of chicken enchiladas. Everyone blesses our newest cooks, and we sit down to eat. Mason excuses himself from the table, and comes back with his mandolin. He asks me to save him some seconds while he plays The Cave for us. He has already learned how to play the song on the guitar, but now that he has his new instrument he was ready to share. My parents says he spent a lot of time listening to that song trying to figure it out on his mandolin.

Cooper is quiet at dinner. I'm not sure what I have done to make him angry, but I figure he will tell me later.

The strange mood Cooper was in continues Monday morning. He joins me for a run and we go our separate ways without a word.

That evening Mason has an away game and our team wins by two goals. Foster starts him in goal, but put him in as a midfielder for the second half, just to see him in action.

The same uncomfortable feeling with Cooper continues on Tuesday.

On Wednesday I didn't send him a text, I decide to run alone. I see him on his deck as I head back home. He sends me a few short texts telling me not to go out alone. I let him know that being alone is better than the awkwardness. He does not respond.

Foster comes over for dinner and goes over plans for our trip. Mason and he have a 4:00 game that day, but we would leave for the airport after Mason hit the shower.

On Thursday, I go for a run without Cooper, again. As I come near his house he meets me.

"Why are you out here alone? You are being childish." I don't answer. I give him a chance to rant and get it off of his chest, so I can continue to run. "Are you not going to say anything?'

"What do you want me to say?"

"Say you won't be out here alone. I don't like it."

"You're not my keeper, protector or brother, Cooper. What's it to you?"

"You matter."

You've got to be kidding me. "You have a funny way to show it." He just stares at me daring me to say something else. "For weeks you act as if I disgust you. You could barely be in the same room without glaring at me, like you're doing right now. We finally began what I thought was friendship only to find you acting like this...again. I'm leaving tonight, so take the next 10 days to figure out if this is going to be friendship or not...because right now I don't understand you."

"I don't understand how you could leave Will's bed, and then sit and talk with me like nothing happened." WHAT?!?!?

I put my hands up and let out a deep breath. When I turn back to him, I still have no words so I just shake my head, and begin to walk off. "What? Nothing to say?" This is beyond frustrating.

"Not that it is your business, but it was my bed not Foster's. I had no problem acting like nothing happened, because NOTHING HAPPENED!!!! FOSTER IS MY FRIEND!!!! He's not my friend with benefits...just friend." I walk away (back home) before Cooper can say anything. After three steps I pick up speed to a full sprint by the time I hit the woods.

Thursday's game goes well, we win by 1 goal. So far 3-0 for the season and our next game is in two weeks.

The rollercoaster of emotions are finally shut out when the plane taxies onto the runway...Europe here we come.

––––––––––

Please vote and/or comment I would like to hear from you.

The Cave video as been posted for this chapter.

Chapter 13 - Leaving your Troubles Behind

The world is a book and those who do not travel read only one page. - St. Augustine Chapter 13 - Leaving Your Troubles BehindMason's POV: We are on our way to the Emirates (Arsenal) stadium to watch Liverpool beat Arsenal. This was pretty much my dad's birthday present for me. I just wish he could be here to share it. It was his idea, but he didn't live long enough to be able to come with us. I miss him. I miss him a lot. Mom is cool though, she was really sad for a while, but she wouldn't talk about dad-so neither did I. It's getting better, but she's still not the mom I knew. She's not as happy as she used to be. Mom brought Coach Foster with us, and even though he was friends with my dad when he was younger...it's not the same. I don't want my mom to replace my dad, but it looks like Coach wants to step into his shoes. I've noticed that as long as I talk with Coach, it keeps him away from my mom. I don't know what Coach is doing. Is he her friend? If so, then he should know she's not ready to forget my dad. So far, Coach has been a decent guy. By the time we checked in at the apartment yesterday Peyton needed a nap. I was tired but I didn't want to waste a day sitting around. So, Coach and I studied the map of the area and found a park near our apartment and decide that would be our resting place. One of the best things in England is that some of the words they use mean something different in the US. Like the park we found was actually a football (soccer) park, and there were a lot of older kids playing. At that moment I was so glad I hadn't forgotten to pack my ball.After Peyton's nap, we traveled back to London. Mom said it was an unusually clear day for March, so our first stop was the London Eye, and then to eat at a pub. I found out something important yesterday. Carrying Peyton around is better than having a puppy. I'm not sure how many girls came up to talk to me, but Peyton and I got a lot of attention from the ladies. Yep, my brother is a chick magnet, and I get to reap the benefit. He was not a bratty little toddler. He's a cool little kid. Something else I noticed yesterday...Coach. I thought he was after my mom, you know friends with benefits, but I don't think he is. He has been treating my mom with a lot of respect, like he wants to be with her and help her just because he wants to, and he doesn't try to do things to make me his buddy. He hugs her a lot, but not in the gross kind of way. They don't kiss in front of me, he might kiss her on the cheek or forehead, but that's all. And that's really good, because my mom doesn't need to be kissing anyone. I also don't think anything nasty is happening with them, my mom looks at him likes he's a buddy. If he wants something else, he may not get it...it looks like he's stuck in the 'friend zone.' I had planned to keep them apart as much as possible during this trip, but considering how they are acting it may be ok."Mason. Come on. This is our stop." Mom smirks at me and Coach when the intercom announces our destination the ends with 'Mind the Gap.' That's London speak for 'watch your step.' I look around at the four of us all decked out in our Liverpool gear. I have my red jacket and beanie, Mom and Peyton are in their sweatshirts, and I gave Coach my dad's hoodie and scarf to wear. I think I shocked him, but he recovered nicely and thanked me. It's just a short walk to my first ever professional soccer game. YES!!!Foster's POV:England has flown by fast; we leave tomorrow for Barcelona. It has been a very busy few days here, but we were able to check off everything on our 'To See' list. Emily spent some time with me talking about Patrick. Even though this trip was supposed to be for Mason, this has been an opportunity for her to heal. I can say she is on the road to recovery. She keeps calling me her lifesaver whenever I take one of the boys with me for a little while. I have kept Peyton while she and Mason go off together, and then she would take Peyton while I'm with Mason. I don't know how she would have handled this trip without help. I know Mason wouldn't have been as happy as he is right now. I let Emily know that she doesn't seem as stressed and tired here as she has been back home. She told me she has been taking something to help her sleep, and that is helping. What I wasn't expecting was that she's had the prescription for a few weeks, but won't take it without another adult around. She is scared that something could happen, and she would not wake up to help her children. She does have quite a few fears about being a single parent, but she is doing a great job.Early this morning I sent Michael and Ms. Hannah an email letting them know about her worries. It seems that someone will have to babysit at Emily's house just so she can sleep. "Can I join you?" Mason asked, breaking me out of my thoughts. He stands by the door to the terrace overlooking the village. "Sure, pull up a seat." He moves over to take the chair beside me. "Are you packed and ready for tomorrow?""Yea sir, this has been fun, but I'm looking forward to the beach and more soccer.""Yeah, me too. That game was good.""Maybe in your world...I thought it was awesome." And there it was, we started talking about the game again. He likes Pepe Reina the keeper for Liverpool, because he was great; but he liked watching Wojciech Szczesny, because he was a showman. I don't think anyone could convince him that Liverpool wasn't the best team, even if there season wasn't going their way.After a comfortable silence Mason asked, "Do you think my mom is going to be ok?""In what way?""You know, with my dad?""Yes I do. She's talking about him more, and not in a sad way."Good was all he added before silence again. This time I spoke first. "I know you miss your dad. So, does your mom." He just smiles at me, but doesn't say anything. I need to talk to him about the possibility of his mom dating. He needs to know that it will happen, and he needs to be ok with that. If she ever remarries, she is not going to be replacing his dad."It's been six months; someday she may be ready to date and find someone who makes her happy." I see him tense."I don't think that she should, I don't want her to. She will forget about my dad.""Her dating doesn't mean she will forget about your dad. Your dad will always be a part of her, and she also has you as a reminder of him. You know she's young, maybe not in your eyes, but she is and she deserves to be happy." I wait for my words to sink in. "When she starts dating, help her. Men are good at hiding their true nature sometimes. If a man bothers you, gives you the creeps, is disrespectful to her or you, tell her. She needs to know. Like if he tries to hard too win you and Peyton over, there might be a problem with him.""Aren't you dating my mom?" He asks, and I had to chuckle."No, Mason. We're just close friends.""So, what are you doing? Scaring off other men?""Maybe something like that. I'm just giving her time to heal, and if that means keeping other men away from her, than yes I am." Mason smiles at me like he approves of my tactics."So, is that why you're always hugging her and kissing her?""You noticed that?""Hard to miss." I laughed at how fast that phrase left his mouth."I love your mom, I always have. I've hugged and kissed on her since she was little. It's just the way we are, but it has only been as friends...no extra benefits.""Even when my dad was around?" "When she started dating your dad...not as much, but I still did. He understood our friendship. He was a good man."Emily's POV:"We're headed out to the beach. Come find us when Peyton wakes up." Foster kisses my forehead before he leaves with Mason. I had warned him that the sunbathers in Barcelona do not like tan lines. He chuckled then stopped when he saw me looking toward Mason. "Oh, got it," was all he replied.I go lay down with my sleeping Peyton. This is the first time in months that I feel at peace. Foster is heaven sent even if he doesn't believe it. I am very thankful he volunteered to come with me. He is fun and fun-loving, but he understands my needs before I do. I don't want to have to lean on him forever. He has his own life, but I'm glad he's with me now.Peyton says, "I wanna go swim."I must have fallen asleep, but I quickly pull my head out of a fog. Peyton brings me his swim trunks, and we change and head off to the beach. Our hotel is on the Las Ramblas near the harbor. It's only a few short blocks to the beach. This is our second day in Barcelona, and I am enjoying the laid back feel of this city. The Las Ramblas is busy with a lot of tourist, but the need to see it all and do it all isn't with us here. Yesterday we walked through the Gothic Quarter just looking at city. The streets in this older part of the city are nothing more than ally ways, and I was surprised that cars actually travel on such narrow streets. After a while we found a few churches to visit, the most beautiful was Santa Anna with the Gothic arches around the courtyard. Foster and Mason had a chuckle at my expense when we found I wasn't dressed appropriately. Foster thought this might have been a first for me. I was dressed in Capri pants and a tank top, but to enter the church my shoulders had to be covered. So, conveniently located outside the church was a little old lady selling scarves...my first souvenir. As Peyton and I walk onto the beach. It's not a crowded as I expected it to be. I see Foster coming from the water. "I'm glad you made it. By the way the water is cold." With that he gives me a big hug and picks me up, completely soaking me."Thanks, I can tell," I say as I push him off of me. Mason takes Foster's lead and repeats the scene, but then decides to shake his wet head and spray me with water in the process."Guys, you could have waited until I stripped down to my swimsuit.""What's the fun in that?" Mason smirks at me and runs back toward the water. "Foster, are you ok?" I ask because his eyes widen and he looks dazed."Emily, you need to put your clothes back on.""Why?" Then I understood and I smile at him. "Thank you.""You look amazing." I know I blushed because I can feel the heat on my face. I feel a rush of excitement as his words register in my brain.I thank him again, and then look at the others at the beach. I feel a little overdressed in my royal blue tankini, while others are in very small bikinis. I also notice that Foster found a place with more families and no nudity...Bravo Foster."Compared to our neighbors, I feel like I'm wearing a muumuu." "On the contrary...modesty is under appreciated, and damn if it's not sexy." With his words I blush again.Foster turns his attention to Peyton, "Come on little man...let's get wet." He takes Peyton by the hand and heads to the water.I can hear Peyton as he touches the water. "It's too cold." It doesn't takes a moment for him to get used to the water, and then he is heading into deeper water with Foster.I am walking to the water's edge when Foster brings Peyton back. "Hey, did you have fun?""The water is cold, Momma.""Do you want to play in the sand with me?""Otay."We are spending time in the sun, burying our feet in the sand when Foster and Mason finally join us. "We built a sand tassel." Peyton tries to castle, but just not quite able to. "Really, was that fun?" Mason asked."Uh huh, wanna do it?""Sure, let's go." Mason moves over a few feet closer to the water to find the best spot to build. Peyton squeals and giggles with his brother as they play in the sand."So, what are our plans for the next few days?" Foster asks."Well, Mumford and Sons concert tonight, and the soccer game is Saturday. I really don't have plans for anything else, but I wouldn't mind going out to the vineyards one day. What about you?""I'm enjoying not having a plan. London wore me out. We were constantly on the go, I like just chillaxing.""Chillaxing...really?" I look at him with a smirk for his made up word."What? It's a word. Isn't it?" I just shake my head at him as he laughs.After a little while we decide to leave the beach and take a longer route back to the hotel looking at new sites.Foster's POV:"Do you want to join me in the lounge? Peyton is asleep, and we won't even leave the hotel...come on." I try to persuade her to go have a drink."Ok, that sounds nice." This is our last night before the reality of home. I tell Mason that we will be downstairs in the hotel lounge. He doesn't care because he too busy Skyping with his friends.We order a bottle of Rioja and a few tapas to share."This has been fun. I think I like the laid back feel of Barcelona more that the hustle and bustle of London," I tell her."I agree." She sits and looks out at the crowd in the Ramblas."I enjoy being busy and in the middle of the excitement, but sometimes it's nice to sit back and be a spectator," she says with a smile."So, what was your favorite part of the trip?""Lionel Messi's legs." I laugh at her answer. I'm not sure if she even watched the game. She mostly stared at Messi."I thought for sure you would like Cristiano Ronaldo.""Do you seriously think Mason could handle me liking someone not on the Barcelona team? I don't think so. By the way Ronaldo's legs are nice, too." She winks at me as she answers, causing me to laugh."Seriously, I liked that you were with me. I couldn't have done this without you. Thanks." She smiles at me and I can't resist kissing her. I press my lips on her temple and just keep the there holding her. "So, what was your favorite?" She asks me.Honestly, I don't know. I loved the games, London, here. Thank you for letting me come with you."We talk for a while about the best parts of the trip, and our plans for the rest of the school year. We are both looking forward to summer break. After a while our conversation becomes more personal."Do you know what scares me the most?" I shake my head at her. "The idea of dating again. I thought I would be married forever. Dating - being with someone new is scary.""Then don't rush it. You're still grieving. Give yourself some time.""Oh, I'm not ready. I'm just saying it scares me. I haven't been on a date with anyone other than Patrick in almost 16 years. I haven't kissed anyone other than him in all that time, and I've only ever been with him."I reach out and take her hand. "It will be alright. Just take your time. I talked with Mason the other night about you dating, again." Her eyes widen. "Don't worry. I let him know that in the future the time may come that you begin dating. He wasn't happy, but he'll be ok." She looks relieved."Thank you. I didn't want to have that talk with him." She pauses for a minute and says, "You know, I'm not ready to move on without him.""But some day you will."

Chapter 14 - Changes in Attitude

Attitude is a little thing that makes a big difference. - Winston Churchill

Chapter 14 - Changes in Attitude

Emily's POV:

Time changes and traveling doesn't help with my inability to sleep. I'm up before dawn waiting for it to be light enough to go to the track. I'm glad to be home, but I'm not looking forward to joining the real world. I took a personal day to recover from this trip, before I go back to the classroom.

Sitting in the living room enjoying the view of the woods, my thoughts wander to all the things I need to do. Laundry, grocery shopping, clothes shopping for the boys, organize summer closets, job hunt for next school year...the list seems endless and overwhelming.

I fumble through my book bag looking for paper and pen to write myself a list of things that needs to be done before tomorrow. I only have this one-day to get as much of this taken care of as possible.

Breathe...breathe. I can feel my heartbeat pounding in my chest. I shake my head to clear my thoughts. Leaving the list on the table, I walk over to the window to watch the sunrise through the trees. It's been a while since I have had a rush of panic, and I wasn't expecting that making plans would bring on such an overwhelming feeling.

Even though it is early, I send a few texts before I forget my thoughts.

I grab my shoes and head out the back door and down the path. As I make it out onto the track I turn up my IPod and find my pace with the music. I'm focusing on my run trying to clear my earlier thoughts. Crap! My knee hits the track hard. I have enough momentum to slide along the ground across my shin. Crap! That burns. The light running pants were not enough protection to keep from scraping my leg from knee to almost ankle.

I bend over and roll up my pant leg. There's not a lot of blood, but the road rash on my shin looks terrible. Securing my pant leg so that I could walk home without the material causing any more irritation, a warm hand touches my shoulder.

"Are you ok?" I look at the hand and then to the face of its owner. "Emily? Oh my, are you ok?"

"Oh my god, I can't believe you're here. What are you doing here?" I stand up and wrap my arms around my friend and he picks me up and gives me a swing. I waited for his answer.

"We'll talk in a minute. Let's get your leg fixed up." I hobble beside him as he walks me a few yards to his house.

He opens the back door and yells, "Hun, you need to come here with the first aid kit. We have an injured guest." No sooner were those words spoken, when Linda Breda comes out the back door with the kit and the biggest hug imaginable.

Tears fill my eyes as I hug my Linda. I've missed her. "I can't believe you're here."

"We just moved in. Garrett starts work next week." She lets me go and looks down at my leg. "That looks awful."

"It feels awful, too." I cringe as she cleans my leg.

"Sorry," she says as he wraps up my leg with gauze.

"It's ok. How long have you guys been here?"

"We bought the house last week. Movers dropped our things off yesterday." Linda looks out passed her backyard and asks, "So, which house is yours?"

"You can't see mine from here, but do you see where the woods begin?" I ask pointing in the direction of my house. "There's a small path that leads to my backyard. It's nice and secluded back there."

She smiles at me. "So, how are you doing?" She asks without the look of pity on her face. Garrett adjusts himself as he also wait for my answer. I feel the need to answer honestly.

"Some days are better than others, but I'm making it." I really don't want to talk about me. I want to find out about my friends.

We spend a little time catching up. Garrett has taken the assignment that was to be Patrick's. Linda is going to be working at Children's Hospital in a few weeks. Their kids, Helen and Edward, will start school tomorrow. Before I leave I invite them for dinner, and I smile as I make my way back home. With Garrett and Linda here, it doesn't feel so much like starting over...just moving on.

I put my phone on the counter as I turn on the water for tea. I have three texts...Michael, Mom, and Cooper.

Michael: I'll come by at 2:00 to discuss finishing the basement.

Mom: Can I use your guestroom for the next few days?

Cooper: I'm glad you're back. Sorry, I couldn't make it for the run. Please tell me you didn't go alone.

Cooper's POV:

Will texted me last night when he and Emily arrived home. I need to talk to Emily. It's been ten days. She told me to figure out what I wanted, and let her know. She was so angry with me when she left, and I was pissed at her, too. I'm over it now, and I missed her.

Emily: Headed out to run.

I smile as I look at my phone. I guess she's not still mad at me. I put on my sweatpants, shirt, sweatshirt and shoes, and head out the back door.

Emily has her arm on the elbow of some guy as she walks toward a house just down from mine. I watch as they reach the back door. I can feel the heat rise up in me. 'What the hell is she thinking? Does she even know this guy? Obviously...'

I watch her stand near his back door. A woman comes out of the house and hugs Emily, and I can here the woman squeal. Ok, I feel better. She does know that man, and he is married...it's ok.

Instead of going back inside, I watch the three of them on the patio. I can only hear garbled sounds, but I see their body language. I feel like an obsessed stalker, but I can't help but watch Emily. I've missed her.

The woman opens a box and puts something on Emily's leg. She's hurt. Her face scrunches up, and then relaxes. I see her. I really see her. She doesn't have make-up on, her hair is pulled up as usual, and she looks like heaven. She wipes her cheeks with her hand, she drops her head, she looks away, she smiles, she relaxes in her seat, she talks, and she smiles some more. I see her...and I feel happy for the first time ten long days.

I grab my phone to text her, as she walks back home.

Me: I'm glad you're back. Sorry, I couldn't make it for the run. Please tell me you didn't go alone.

Emily: It's ok. I cut the run short.

Me: I'd like to talk to you soon. Lunch?

Emily: Sounds good. Where?

Me: My house, noon.

Emily: See you then.

Emily's POV:

Not wanting to try to read between the lines, I opted to call Mom instead of text. "Mom, no. It's fine. It's easier for you to stay here if you and Dad are going to be working at Foster's house. What does he have you doing, anyway?" I ask.

"He has a small project. Since your dad retired, he needs things to keep himself busy. Those are his words, not mine."

"What time will you be here?"

"Your dad just loaded up the tractor, and we will be on our way as soon as we pack a few things. Maybe 12:30-1:00."

"Sounds good. I won't be here, but Mason will."

"Are you running errands?"

"No, I'm finished doing that. I'm meeting Cooper for lunch, and taking Peyton with me."

"Hmmm," was all she said, but it was the tone that bothered me.

"Hmmm, what?"

"Hmmm, nothing. I love you... I'll see you later." With that she hung up.

I pull the suit case into the laundry room, and start a load of clothes. The boys were upstairs gathering all of the dirty clothing that has yet to be brought to me. This has been a busy morning, with still more to do before we go back to school tomorrow.

Dishes are drying, a second load of clothes are washing, and I roll the vacuum cleaner back into the closet...done for a little while.

"Peyton, do you want to go with me?"

"Yea, where we go?" He is still making short sentences, but the upturned hands and shoulder shrug that goes with the question is adorable.

"We are going to Cooper's house."

"I wanna see Addy."

"No, Peyton. Addy is at school today."

"Oh"

I put my shoes on, and check my appearance in the mirror. Not too bad. I apply a fresh coat lip gloss and powder down my shine, and then call upstairs to let Mason know we were leaving.

I pull the stroller out of the garage, but Peyton wants to hold my hand as we walk the track to Cooper's house. It occurs to me this will be the first time I have been in his house. I've been to his house, but I've never had a reason to go inside.

Peyton's walking expedition didn't last long. By the time we made it to Cooper's backyard, Peyton decided it was too far and wanted to ride. "Hey Emily, I see you brought reinforcements."

"Yes, just in case truce talks broke down and we were at a standstill." Cooper laughs good maybe this will go ok.

"Come on in, I brought something from Tia's Deli. I hope that's ok."

"That sounds great. Wow, Cooper your house is beautiful. It's like a museum." I smile at him, but this house is quite a show piece. It had an open floor plan with a formal living room and dining room, a family room and an impressive kitchen all sporting 12 to 14 feet ceilings. There were columns and archways helping to divide the rooms, but each room was really open to the next. The walls were colored dark rich tones, with dark wood furniture that were each works of art. As beautiful as it was, it made me feel uncomfortable. I felt a bit intimidated to touch anything, and I kept Peyton in my arms.

I follow Cooper as he goes to the kitchen to gather plates, cups, and silverware. We sit at a small table in the hearth room. The space is more cozy and intimate than the rest of the house. "This is my favorite room," he says as he smiles at me.

The room has a stone fireplace and walls painted a warm golden green. "I can see why. It's very homey."

"My thoughts exactly. The rest of the house is a too stiff." I didn't know if I was allowed to agree, so I just smile. We ate in silence, because I am too scared to begin the conversation that I know needs to happen.

"I'm sorry," he says, and I look at him. "I've missed you. I'm sorry for getting mad at you for something that didn't happen, but also was none of my business."

My heart was lifted, and feels like it could soar. "I'm sorry, too."

"What do you have to be sorry about?"

"I'm sorry I didn't understand why you were upset at me earlier. This could have been avoided, if we would have talked." I gave him a weak smile hoping that he understood that he can talk to me about almost anything.

"No, you were right. It's none of my business. I just didn't...don't want to see you hurt."

"Well, I can put your mind at ease. Foster will not hurt me." I continue to talk to him about Foster and what had happened that night and the next day. My words are making him feel uncomfortable, but not because of the events. Cooper jumped to the wrong conclusion without giving me or Foster any benefit of doubt. I can tell I was tried and found convicted in Cooper's eyes, and he now feels guilty for his own actions.

"From now on, no more Mr. Moody Cooper. If you have a problem with me, use your words. Talk to me. I may get mad, but at least I will know what you are thinking. We may even be able to clear the air."

"OK." He takes my hand in his, and my heart begins to race. I look at our hands, and then search his face for what he is thinking. I can't read it. It looks no different than it did a few minutes ago. He doesn't seem to be affected by the touch like I am. I look back at our hands and blow out a breath. He thinks we're friends, then friends we will be.

"Are you ready to go back to work tomorrow?"

"NOOO!" He laughs, but I'm quite serious. I don't want to go. "Only 45 more days 'til summer...not that I'm counting."

Cooper's POV:

I reach out to take Emily's hand, and she lets me. She looks at me, and I can't help but get lost in her eyes. Damn, I sound like a school girl with her first crush. This is just a woman. Umm, but man is she a woman.

She helps me clean up from lunch, and I place my hand on her back and walk her out to the track. We walk together until she comes to the path that leads her home. "Would you like to come over for dinner? My parents are staying with me for a few days, and I have some people I would like you to meet. If you don't mind a crowd, I would like for you and Addy to come."

"Yes. I would like that."

Emily picks up Addy afterschool for me, since I seem to be without a babysitter, again. When I get to her house, it looks like a party.

"It's about time you got here, son." Jim, Emily's father, greets me at the door. I can see Will, Michael, and the man from this morning are talking on the back deck. Emily, Ms. Hannah, Keira, and the woman from this morning are in the kitchen setting out food.

"Hi, I'm glad you made it." Emily smiles at me, and I get lost in her eyes. "I would like you to meet my friends. This is Linda Breda. Her husband and Patrick have had three assignments together. They just moved in yesterday. Linda this is Cooper Mills."

"Nice to meet you." I reach out my hand to shake. She seems friendly, but much older than Emily.

"Come with me. I would like you to meet her husband." I follow her out to where the men have gathered. "Garrett this is my friend Cooper Mills. He's Addy's uncle. Cooper this is Garrett Breda."

Garrett reaches for my hand. "I've been enjoying watching your little Addy. She and Helen have hit it off quite nicely." I follow his eyes out to the backyard where Emily's sons, nephews, Chandler and some other boy are playing soccer, and there on the sidelines is little Addy and cute little brown haired girl playing cheerleaders.

"Oh, heaven help us," I mumble, he just shakes his head and chuckles. So, this is the man that helped Emily on what was probably the worst night of her life. The night she found out her husband was dead.

Jim and CJ call for the kids to come in for dinner, as they take the rest of the food off the grill. Funny, in all this chaos I didn't even notice CJ was here.

Finding a place to sit and eat was a bit more challenging than usual. Emily has the kitchen counter, dining room table, patio table and coffee table filled with dinner plates. She is in her element playing hostess for us all.

It is a little crowded, but no one seems to mind. I can't help but feel happy when I'm here, even with this many people.

"Do you have plans this weekend?" Will asks me.

"No."

"Good, let's go to Jonesboro. I want to watch some rugby. Arkansas State is ranked number one in the nation. I want see them in action." I shake my head at him. I can't believe him.

"What? Summer is baseball, fall is football, winter is basketball, and that leaves spring for soccer and rugby."

"What about hockey?"

"If I knew where to watch a hockey game around here, I'd go." Will looks at me in complete seriousness.

"We need to see if Emily wants to go." He says as he turns to her.

"She'll want to go watch rugby?" I ask. Will laughed like he had a secret.

"Emily, A-State rugby is playing at home this Saturday. Do you want to go?"

"Sure, we can take my vehicle." She smiles at Will and then me. I'll be damned, she didn't even flinch.

Please vote and comment. I am looking forward to hearing from you.

Chapter 15 - Mini Road Trip

M y other life keeps me calm and grounded and normal. - Shawn Johnson

Chapter 15 Mini-Road Trip

Cooper's POV:

"Good morning, Ms. Hannah," I say as Emily's mom meets me at the door. Addy runs past me to find Mason.

"Emily's running around here somewhere with Peyton. She'll be back in a minute. Coffee?"

"Thanks." I follow her to the kitchen, grab coffee, and talk to Ms. Hannah. She is happy that I started taken off work on Saturdays. She thinks I'm missing too much of Addy's life by working all the time. My phone chirps with a text.

Will: Change of plans. Swing by and pick us up...bring Hannah with you.

I let Ms. Hannah know that Will wants her to come to his house. She says that will save Jim a trip to come back and pick her up.

Mason walks in pours a glass of milk, and offers a glass to Addy. They are an unlikely pair. He calls her squirt, and that earns him a scowl. I'm busy watching when I hear a soft chuckle behind me.

"Good morning, Cooper." I turn around and I had to catch my breath. Emily smiles at me with Peyton in her arms.

"Good morning." I reach out and touch her hand. I've spent every evening with her this week, and I still can't keep it together when she's in the room.

"What?" She twists her forehead, and searches my face. "I'm wearing school colors. I don't have an A-State shirt, but I have red and black."

"You look nice." Look nice? She's wearing a red fitted t-shirt, a pair of slim black pants that hit a few inches above the ankle, and black and gray sandals. She has her hair braided to one side, and she looks like a college kid. I know she's close to 30, but she looks like she shed 8-10 years off of her age. Her clothes hug her small body and show off her slim curves, and I need to turn my head to keep from staring.

"You ok?" My eyes jerk toward the kitchen. Ms. Hannah is grinning at me, and I just nod.

"Don't worry Mom, that's just Cooper. He does that a lot." What? I do what a lot? Emily leans down, "You were staring at me weird again," and then she grins and tries to walks off.

"Coop, I want Coop." I reach out for Peyton and he crawls into my lap.

"You ready for our big day?" He nods.

"Are you sure you don't want me to keep him with me?"

"No, Momma, He'll be fine. We are only going to the game. He will like it. It's not like a football game, there is areas for the kids to run around if we need it."

She turns her attention from her mom to me. "Could you grab the ice chest and put it in the back of the vehicle?" She tosses me her keys. "By the way, do you mind driving?" It's only about a 2 hour trip, and I don't mind being the driver.

"No, that's fine." She busies herself with bags and sends Mason and Addy out with their hands full.

Will is standing in the driveway when we get to his house. He barely says hello as he makes a beeline to Emily. "I need you to see something." He helps her out and they walk together to the back of his house. Before I could round the corner, I hear her squeal.

"You did this?" She looks from Will to her dad. "Was this your idea?" Will nods and she throws her hands around his neck. She looks so happy as her eyes meet mine. She becomes more serious as she looks back at Will, "You made room for me at your house." Her eyes fill with tears as Will kisses her forehead.

"I sure did." I feel a stab in my chest. I watch him reach down and pick her up as she buries her face in his neck. I want to go tear them apart, but I know this is just how they are together...just friends.

I look past the hugging couple and take in Will's new backyard. Jim has dug up the backyard to install a swimming pool, volleyball net and court, and raised garden beds.

"I haven't had a vegetable garden in years. I can't believe you did this."

"Really, woman, you notice the garden and not the pool and court? Really?" Will is laughing at her.

"Yes." She crinkles up her nose, "the pool and court are for everyone, and it's quite nice. But, I know you only put in the garden because of me." And then, she burst out laughing. "I love it."

She walks over to the beds with Addy, I guess they are discussing what is going to be planted. Peyton, Mason and Chandler walk to the pool. "Will, you did good." He gives me a cocky smirk, and looks quite proud of himself.

"Jim, Ms. Hannah, this yard looks great. You did a fantastic job." They are just happy that the kids like it as much as they do. They say their 'thank you's come in the form of smiles.

I drive in relative silence. Will is sitting shotgun, Emily behind me, Peyton beside her, and the three older kids in the back watching Ironman2 ... Mason's choice. I can see everyone through the mirror, but my eyes keep finding Emily.

Will decides to play 'music appreciation' with his IPod, which translates to us dealing with whatever he decides to play. Since Emily wasn't much for country music that's what he chooses.

"You catching up on sleep, yet?" Will asks as he turns back to talk to Emily.

"Yeah, I'm sleeping more than six hours a night now." She smirks at him. "I guess this was your idea, to get my parent to stay so I'll take my pill." What? I look over at Will as he feigns innocence.

"What's going on? What pills?"

"My doctor prescribed sleeping pills. No biggie."

"Only she won't take them if she's the only adult in the house." I glance back at Emily as she looks out the window instead of at Will. "In case something happens, she doesn't want Mason to have the burden of taking care of everything." He turns his attention back to her. "Don't worry Michael and I have worked out a schedule for the next week. Two if you need it."

"Thanks," was all she said, but I can tell it bothers her to need help.

The rugby field is located at the edge of the campus, and has a few small sets of bleachers. The crowd is not much larger than a high school soccer or baseball game, but that's what happens in the south. If it's not football...no one really notices.

Emily gathers Peyton's diaper bag and a few bottles of water and walks ahead with Addy, holding Peyton's hand. She suddenly stops and bends down to talk with Peyton, and then she turns to me with a huge smile.

"You can ask him," she says as she smiles back at Peyton.

"Coop, can I hold you?" Peyton asks as he holds up both hands toward me.

"Sure, little man, you can hold me." I couldn't hold back my smile...Peyton wants me. Emily walks beside me, and I reach out to take her hand.

"Momma, Coop is holding me." He announces and pats my shoulder.

I haven't watched rugby since I was in college. It took a little while to remember some of the rules. It wouldn't matter if I had ever seen a game, it's fast and exciting. Fun as he'll to watch.

A couple of minutes into the game, Will hands me a napkin to give to Emily. "What's this for?"

"Trust me, just give this to her."

I reach forward and hand her the napkin, and she looks at me curiously. "It's from Will."

He bursts out laughing, and she scowls so hard that I can't help but chuckle. "Emily, seriously you need to wipe up the drool." I shoot him a look.

"Foster, you're funny," she says sarcastically, but she didn't look as pissed as I thought she was going to. She softens her look into something resembling a sweet thoughtfulness. "This is by far my favorite sport now...thanks for the short shorts." And then she waggles her eyebrows and laughs.

Will elbows me, "She likes legs. I knew she would like rugby, even if it was only for the uniform." He could not be serious.

At half-time two college boys sat down, one beside Emily the other in front of his friend. Emily didn't seem to notice them as she was watching Peyton and Addy walking around near the bleachers. As she turns around the boy beside her tries to strike up a conversation. I am about to interfere, but Will stops me. "This will be funny. These guys have no clue." I decide to sit back and watch, knowing I can put a stop to this anytime I need to.

"So, is this your first game? I haven't seen you before." Guy number one doesn't sound like an American. He's tall, blonde, and looks like an athlete, but clearly from another country.

"This is my first game. I usually watch other sports."

"Like what?"

"Soccer mostly, but baseball and football." She smiles at him, but in a curious way...not like she's interested.

"Where I'm from soccer is football." He smirks hoping his accent and his being from another country is a plus.

"Yes, I know...but here in the US it's called soccer so the fans don't get confused." She giggles and cuts her eyes to Will. It must be some sort of inside joke.

"I'm from South Africa. We don't play American football there." I tune out the conversation because I can only see Emily. She is polite even though she would like to keep an eye on our kids.

For the rest of half-time boy wonder number one continues to flirt and get the attention of Emily. She is polite, but gives him no encouragement to continue his pursuit. "That's what she's always like. She can read it when it happens to someone else, but not to her. She has no clue this guy is trying to pick her up, and he doesn't know what to do to get her attention. It's funny. It always has been." He looks me in the eyes and says, "You're smart, you're being her friend first, but you're going to have to tell her how you feel. She won't know unless you do. She doesn't see herself as anything other than a friend when it comes to most guys, mostly because any guy that showed her any attention when she was young was run off by her brothers or cousins. Patrick was the exception. I don't think he ever let her think of him as anything other than her future from the moment they met."

I look back at her. "I know what you're feeling. I can see it in the way you look at her. You're my friend, but you hurt her...we're done." There is nothing to say to that, because I'm sure what I'm feeling...but hurting her isn't going to be part of it.

Will smirks at me, "Let's put the guys out of their misery, shall we?" He leaves and picks up Peyton and brings him back to the bleachers.

"Hey, sweetie, let the tiger bait go. You're son needs his sippy cup." She reaches for Peyton, and the boys look astonished.

"You have a kid?" Tiger bait one asks.

"Yes, two of them." Right on cue Mason shows up and sits on the other side of his mom.

"Hey, Mom, can I have the key to get something from the truck?" The look on the faces of these two college boys is priceless, and earns a very loud laugh from Will and me.

She looks back at us and realizes what is happening, "Oh my god, I feel like a cougar."

"Emily, you're not old enough to be a cougar, yet. You're more like a Puma," Will says with a laugh.

"Thanks."

Boy wonder (tiger bait) beside her asks how old she was, and she declines revealing that information. She did get him to tell her he was 21, and he was hoping she was 22 or 23. She let him know that adding 10 years to that number was closer to her age. Damn, she's older than 33. I can't help but smile, she closer to my age than I thought.

This is unedited...written fast before my thoughts could be interupted.

Please vote and/or comment. I look forward to hearing from you.

Chapter 16 - She Needs Help

We can't help everyone, but everyone can help someone - Ronald Reagan

Chapter 16 – She Needs Help

Emily's POV:

Linda: Tomorrow night 7:00 – we'll pick you up

Me: Fine

Linda: Don't sound so happy about it

Me: This is me being happy

Before she can send me a snappy comeback...

Me: Gotta go...see ya soon

With that I put me phone back in my pocket as I wait with Addy and Helen for Cooper to arrive for lunch. Helen is not one of my students. When she started school, she was placed in Lillian's room. She and Addy have been pretty much been inseparable since she has moved in almost six weeks ago. This is our last Friday lunch together, so Cooper is bringing in their favorite…bacon, lettuce, and tomato sandwiches with salt and vinegar chips.

"How are my favorite girls?" Cooper asks as he waltzes in with his boxes of lunch goodies for us.

Addy and Helen immediately start zombie walking toward him, "Food…food…give us food." They smile and bat their eyes eyelashes at him, "Thanks, Uncle Cooper."

I thank him for lunch, and he sits down beside me across from the girls. I watch him as he takes a visual inventory of my classroom. "It's changed a lot since the last time I was in here."

"Good or Bad?"

"Neither…different. Not as busy." Well, it is the end of the school year. I can't keep the decorations up over the summer. In fact, I can't keep them up at all; I'll be leaving at the end of this year. I haven't told anyone, yet, but I have not accepted the permanent position that was offered. I won't be returning next year.

"I've been taking down some of the decorations, preparing for summer. I'm only keeping up what is needed for lessons. I sort of like it better this way. Cleaner walls feel calmer, and when I'm teaching a bunch of 10 year old…I need some calm." I smile waiting for the inevitable retort from the kiddos in the room.

"What? I don't understand, we're not calm?" Helen does a surprise gasp of innocence. "We are always calm…like a lullaby." Addy burst out laughing.

"Yeah, that's us. A lullaby." They both laugh even louder.

The girls entertain us with stories of their friends, and class, and plans for this coming weekend. Addy throws away her lunch trash and comes over to rest her chin on my shoulder. This has been a common action here and at home, and I reach up and touch her cheek. Helen cannot be outdone, so she takes a place in my lap...which is how she has always been with me even in California.

"You look loved." Cooper says with a smirk.

"Oh, I feel loved." I roll my eyes at him, and he chuckles. "Girls, Cooper, if you will excuse me. I need to take the class out to recess. I'll be right back."

The girls try to go with me, and I look at Addy, "Your Uncle Cooper is here to see you. Why don't you stay here with him, and I will be back in a few minutes."

I walk back to my classroom trying to gather my thought for what could be a difficult conversation.

"Ok, Addy and Helen, it's time for recess. The class is already on the playground. I'll see in a little while." They say goodbye, and are out the door.

"Alright let me have it." He smirks at me. He must be better at reading me than I am at reading him. "I can see the teacher look on your face. So, what's going on?" I let out a little breath...here goes.

"I need to talk to you as Addy's teacher for a minute. I don't want to overstep my bounds, but as her teacher we need to talk." He gives me a small smile.

"It's ok. Tell me what's going on."

"First of all this is not academic...it's social. She doesn't know I'm talking to you about this, but she's growing. She has needs that she may not feel comfortable talking about with her uncle." I give him a pointed look hoping that he catches a clue of what I am trying to say to him. He doesn't. "Her body is changing, and she is asking questions. Unfortunately, she's asking friends not adults." Again, I'm trying not to have to say this. Then, he catches on.

"Oh."

"Yes, oh. She needs someone to talk to. I know Foster has his mom to help with Chandler. Do you have someone that can talk to Addy?" He smiles and then it turns into a smirk. I don't change my expression. I'm not here at his buddy Emily. I'm here for Addy. He needs to know the seriousness of this conversation.

"Well, I know this nice lady in my neighborhood." Again, I don't change me expression.

"I'm serious. She needs someone to talk to...someone who will answer her questions. Help her."

He reaches out for my hand and rubs my knuckles with his thumb. I watch his hand as he does this. Does he know what this feels like to me? I look up to see his beautiful, blue eyes as he studies my face. His expression has changed to one of concern.

"Emily, I am serious. She likes you, she trusts you. I trust you...do you mind helping her? If she feels uncomfortable talking with me, then I would prefer she talks to you."

"Thank you for your trust. I would be honored." I let out a breath. While the irons are hot, "Now I need to take Addy shopping." He lets out a huge laugh.

"Shopping, really."

"Well yeah, unless you want to help her with buying her first bra." He lets out a groan and looks like he just aged ten years...priceless. I pat the top of his hand. "You'll be ok. You will make it through this."

"I need a subject change, fast." He lets out a deep breath. "You didn't answer me this morning about watching the Travs tomorrow night."

I smile, but I know it probably looks more like a grimace. "As much as I like sports, I'm going to have to pass on watching a Travelers play." I'm not ready to start up with minor league ball. "Do you or Foster know I'm a girl? I don't think my brothers do, but I was hoping you or Foster would."

"What is that supposed to mean? Of course, I know you're a girl."

"Really? Please tell me how we have spent the last few weeks? At least a dozen soccer games, not including Mason's, three rugby games, four baseball games...high school and college, and now minor league baseball? I don't think so." I know I sound like a bitch, but I'm tired of being one of the boys. "I know you guys keep asking me so I'm not sitting around moping, and I love you for it. But I think I'm ready to go out on a date. It would be nice to go to a concert, dinner, or a movie...something not sports for a change." He looks happy for me. I'm glad, because I'm scared to death.

"Linda has fixed me up on a blind date. She and Garrett are going to double." Ok, now he doesn't look happy. Great, now bodyguard Cooper is about to come out to play. I just shake my head. He's about to go all caveman/big brother on me, and I am going to cut off. "She's been trying to do this for a couple of weeks. It's about time I get out there. It's been almost 9 months, and you guys can't babysit me forever. You have your own life; it's not fair for me to keep you from it."

I can tell he wants to tell me something, but I timed this conversation to my advantage. "Oh, look at the time. I need to go get the kids from recess." He didn't say anything as we went our separate ways.

Check out my picture of Addy.

Please don't hate me. Vote and/or comment...but not hate.

Chapter 17 - Just Like That

"Girls you've gotta know when it's time to turn the page." —— Tori Amos

Chapter 17 - Just Like That

Emily's POV:

I have the weekend to myself. My dad and Michael have been working on a project in my basement. After Mason walked Addy home, my dad took the boys with him for a few days.

Yesterday morning I woke up ready to make a change. For the last few weeks, Linda had been trying to set me up on a date with one of her co-workers. I kept declining. I was happy in my 'non-dating -- guys as friends' life, until I saw the pitied look Cooper gave me, or at least thats what it looks like to me. I see it from Foster, too, but not as much. They have been wonderful about not letting me mope, but I can't be their charity case forever. I need to learn to help myself. I need to start my life without Patrick, and dating is the next step.

As much as I love Foster and even Cooper, I'm tired of feeling like they're waiting for me to get better. So, I actually woke up yesterday and decided I didn't want to feel like this anymore and not ever again. So. I'm changing, just like that...I take a step to better. I accepted Linda's double date...

Foster came by last night to talk with me.

"You drinking alone tonight, too?"

"Not if you're joining me." He looks at my patio table and surveys the dirty dishes I have yet to pick up.

"Whatever you're drinking, you look better than Cooper." I ignore his comment. I don't need a lecture from him or Cooper tonight, and I really don't care how mad Cooper is at me. He should be happy I'm taking this step.

"Port. Have you ever had any?

"No." I go get a glass and a small plate of chocolate and fruit.

"I'm glad you're here. This is my last bottle, and I'm glad I can share it with you." I give him a smile that I hope looks genuine. I've been throwing myself a pity party, and I don't want him to think he is not welcome here. "Patrick and I bought is in Napa Valley on vacation last spring. We had never had port wine, and a man from Rutherford Hills has us taste it." I nod for him to take a sip. I giggle at his twisted, grimaced face. "That was my first thought, too. The man said it tasted so much better with dessert, and he handed us chocolate covered blueberries." I hand him the same. "Now, take another sip."

"Oh my god, I just fell in love."

"I know my thoughts exactly. Needless to say we bought six bottles." I hold up the half empty bottle. "But this is the last of it. We planned on going back to Napa before we moved here, but that didn't happen." I could feel tears sting my eyes, but for once I didn't try to stop them.

Foster moves to a seat closer to me, after he kissed my forehead. He reaches over to hold my hand. He didn't say anything, he just let me cry.

"I accepted a date."

"I know. Cooper told me."

"Are you about to go all bodyguard/protector on me?"

"No, I'm just checking on you. Trying to find out where your head is." His eyes feel like they are burning through my skin.

"My head is firmly on my shoulders. Linda and Garrett are doubling with me, so I'm not alone with a stranger." I smirk at him, "Is that ok daddy?"

"Oooooo, Daddy?" He smirks and chuckles. I shouldn't have gone there. "I like it. Who's your daddy?" His wiggles his body in an odd attempt at being suggestive. I just shake my head at him. My tears are drying up, but mostly because Foster has a wonderful way of lightening the mood.

"So, you think you're ready for this?"

"I don't know. Part of me is, the other part wants to crawl up in a hole." He squeezes my hand and I give him a weak smile. "I made a vow to myself. I hate the way I've been feeling. I'm going to do what I can to change that." I could immediately see his wheel spinning.

I give him a questioning look and ask, "Therapy?"

"You read my mind," he says as he smiles at me.

"The last session was this past Monday. I can come back if I need; I've joined a support group."

"Meds?"

"I was given an anti-anxiety med for my panic attacks. I only take it when I need it, and I have only needed it once...so far."

"Good girl, you're right. Your head is on your shoulders." He leans over and kisses my temple. "You waited unil you were ready, instead of jumping in because you're lonely."

After a few minutes of silence I whisper, "Am I making a mistake? Is it too soon?"

With a squeeze of my hand, "Only you can answer that."

"Thanks." We sat in silence for a long time, as I thought about what tomorrow holds. "I'm not just doing this for me. I'm doing this for my boys and for your and for Cooper."

"Me and Cooper?" I smile at him even though I know it is weak. "Don't think for a minute Cooper didn't give me every detail of your lunch today." I know I looked panicked because he chuckles and squeezes my hand again.

"Is he mad? I didn't give him a chance to say anything."

"No, he's not mad." For the first time, I can see Foster has lied to me. I don't know if I can take another bout of Moody Cooper.

"Don't lie to me. I can see it in your face." He looks directly into my eyes. "Believe me; he is not mad at you." Ok, I can tell he told me the truth, but he is hiding something.

"I'm scared about tomorrow." He pulls me over closer and puts his arm around me.

"Don't be. First off, this really isn't a date. It's a meeting. You're just meeting someone new. Second, you'll have Linda and Garrett to help if it gets awkward. Third, be yourself. He's going to love you." Even though I find comfort in his words, I can't help but shed some more tears.

"Woah, what are these for?" Foster asks as he wipes my tears from my cheeks. The concern in his voice was overwhelming, and I loose my battle with the sobs that have not been heard in almost 9 months.

Foster pulls me into his lap and I bury my head in his neck and cry.

Today has been busy. This morning I spent some time cleaning the house. Without the boys here I was able to start Saturday chores early. I did take a sleeping pill, for the first time in weeks, to make sure I got enough sleep. I knew my thoughts of my date would keep me from being able to relax.

Girls' night this month turned out to be girls' day at the spa.

Lillian, being a sucker for new romance, wanted to know about my date tonight.

"Ok, girl spill." Her eyes are wide and ready to absorb all of the details.

"There's nothing to tell."

"Oh no, you're not getting away with that."

"Really, I don't know much. I don't even know his name." She looks at me like I have grown a third head. "Linda assures me he is nice. She says he has a good bedside manner."

"Hmmm, bedside manner on a date is good." Ericka chimes in. I roll my eyes at her and she bursts out laughing.

"He's a doctor. The nurses call him Dr. Eye-Candy." I twist my face. "All I can think is - arrogant man who thinks he's God's gift to women."

"Way to be positive," Lillian says. "Any other details?"

"Not really...dark hair, about 5'9", stunning smile, and a dimple on the right cheek." I roll my eyes. "Linda keeps teasing me with information, but without a name, it's meaningless."

Robyn and Ericka have dreamy looks on their faces. "Either one of you want to take my place?"

"No, but if you don't want him, I call dibs." Robyn says then high fives Lillian.

"Ok, so where are you going?"

"Don't know."

"What do you know? We want details."

"I'm meeting Linda, Addy and Helen later to go shopping. I guess I'll get details then. It would be nice to know what to wear."

I bid the girls goodbye after a manicure and pedicure. I stay longer for a facial and a haircut.

I usually wear my hair up to keep it from bothering me as I work. I enjoy the different styles having long hair provides, but I want something else for tonight.

My hair has grown very long. My stylist and I decide to cut it to where it hits at the bottom of my shoulder blades with a few long layers. I watch as my hair hits the floor...more than 6 inches off. He styles it letting my natural curl shape my face. He offers to do my make-up. He thinks I have beautiful eyes that need to be played up. "Your eyes look like they are taking in the world. They are begging men to get lost in them." I laugh, but he does show me how to play up my eyes even more for the night.

I meet up with the girls to shop for new clothes.

"You look amazing," Linda says as I reach the mall entrance.

"You're beautiful," Addy adds and beams a giant smile at me. "Wait 'til Uncle Cooper sees you."

"Thanks."

Time to get down to business...little girl shopping. We start with bras, and then we began looking for summer clothes: shorts, shirts, capris, and dresses. Helen and Addy are hilarious to watch. They keep coming up with little chants and cheers, and they have a distinct style when it comes to clothes...cute but comfortable. They will bypass cute for comfort no matter what.

"You never told me where we were going. I need to know how to dress."

"We're eating a Bosco's by the River Market and then we may go to Creegan's for drinks." I blow out a breath. "I'm wearing a dress, probably a red sheath."

"I'll need to get something. None of my dresses fit. I tried a few things on last night...nothing looks good."

"Girl, you've lost a lot of weight that you couldn't afford. I bet not much in your closet fits anymore."

I just shake my head. She' s right. Most of my clothes hang on me, but I have some clothes that fit good enough.

She and the girls help select a few dresses for me to try. Hot pink, purple, royal blue, black, silver...you name it the girls find it. I nix many of the dresses on color alone. I pick one dress, a-line, halter, at the knee, fitted waist, and low back...best of all blue...soft ocean blue. As soon I put it on, I knew I have a winner. The looks on Linda's and the girls' faces confirms that I have found my dress. Sexy and understated...just the way I like it.

As soon as I pull up into Cooper's driveway, Addy runs into the house, leaving me to gather today's booty. I hear her yelling, "You got to see Ms. Cahill. She's beautiful." I can hear Cooper's response, "She's always beautiful."

"Not like this." I walk into the living room and put down the shopping bags. I hear Cooper catch his breath. I smile to myself. 'Did I cause that?'

He looks straight into my eyes with an expression I haven't seen before. "Beautiful doesn't even come close to describing the way you look." I feel heat rise to my face. "Your hair...I just want to touch it. I've never seen it down. Amazing," he whispers, and almost looks in awe.

Addy squeals, "Kiss her, You need to kiss her." I feel more heat rise up. My face is burning...kiss me.

Cooper leans toward me, moving his eyes from mine to my lips. My breath hitches and so does his. He presses his lips to the corner of my mouth, and he lets out a slow breath.

"Happy? I kissed her." Addy was elated, and I was, for lack of a better word, confused. She took her bags and left the room. "I'll leave you two alone now. My job here is done."

Cooper is still close to me. He moves his hand up and runs his fingers though my hair. "Beautiful is just not a good enough word to describe you." I look at him. "Thanks." Then, he takes a step back, and I miss the feel of him.

"Thank you for taking her shopping. How was it? Is she all set?" There it is again...friend. I shake my thoughts of Cooper away, and begin telling him about mine and Addy's day. He thanks me for taking care of her, but it truly is no trouble. I love that little girl.

Now here I am ready to go on a first date for the first time in over 16 years. I take my wedding ring from the chain I have been wearing, and place them in a black velvet box and close the lid.

Nervous as hell...and there is the doorbell....time to go.

There may be many errors. I haven't checked, yet.

Please vote and/or comment.... I love to hear from you.

A picture of Emily's dress is posted.

Chapter 18 - The Next Step to Normal

I had origanlly written the Spanish part with an English translation, but was told it was hard to follow. So, instead the italicized words indicate a Spanish conversation. Also, I posted a picture of my inspriation for Emily's date. Enjoy!

Hope is a waking dream. - Aristotle

Chapter 18 - The Next Step to Normal

Emily POV:

Linda grabs my hand as we walk up the stairs to the restaurant. "You'll be ok." I nod letting her know I hear her words.

"Garrett, we'll meet you at the table. We're going for a pit stop first." She kisses his lips softly and walks away with me.

As soon as the door shuts to the bathroom, she turns to me and says, "I know you're about to panic. I see it in your face, and hear it in your breath." I smile weakly at her because all I was telling myself was...breathe....breathe. I knew it was coming.

She gives me a few minutes to get myself together. "Do you have your medication with you?" I nod. "Don't take it, yet. Give yourself a few minutes at the table. If you feel this again, we'll excuse ourselves to take your pill." I smile weakly again, and then agree. I don't want to ruin this night for anyone, but maybe it is too soon.

Boscos is a very nice first class restaurant known for its handcrafted beer. It is a quiet comforting place to have a very relaxing dinner. CJ and Keira have taken me here in January to get me out of my house for a little while. I love this place.

Entering the main dining room, Linda finds Garrett and I follow them to our table. My date has his back to the room. He has dark hair and wide shoulders. I can see the muscles, but he's more toned than large. I watch him as he turns around to meet us. I whisper to Linda, "You got me a date with Dr. Studly?" I look at her in complete astonishment. She seems very proud of herself. "Why didn't you tell me?"

"I didn't want to. I thought you would accept a date when you were ready."

"I'm not sure I am."

"But you accepted. That's a huge step forward for you."

Dr. Gavin Roberts stood waiting at our table for us to arrive. Gavin Roberts who was nicknamed Dr. Studly by all the moms in my old neighborhood. Gavin Roberts who was my neighbor in California, and who was Mason's pediatrician for almost 3 years. Dr. Gavin Roberts who had lost his wife over a year ago to ovarian cancer. Dr. Gavin Roberts - one of the most stunning men I have ever met, and he is my date for the evening.

"Put your eyes back in your head, girl." Linda giggles beside me. I laugh but keep my eyes glued on the man before me. The pewter gray shirt makes his eyes sparkle. He stands and his body is a perfect manly triangle...wide shoulders, broad chest, and narrow hips. I never truly noticed how very delicious he was. I blush as my thoughts of him run wild through my imagination.

"Emily, I'm so glad you finally accepted my offer of a date. Granted Linda wouldn't give me your number so I could ask you directly." He glares at Linda; who is smiling trying to look innocent. He takes my hand and pulls me closer, and then kisses each side of my face. "You look lovely," he whispers.

"Thank you." I lean back to take in the full effect of Gavin's beauty. "It seems Linda is up to something. She wouldn't even tell me whom she was setting me up with. This must be a game to her." Linda just shakes her head.

"If I would have told you, Emily. You would have accepted this date as a buddy hang-out session, not as a real date which is what this is." She challenges me with her look, but I know that is exactly what I would have done. If nothing else, Gavin and his late wife Stacy were neighbors and friends. I would have come on a date just to catch up with an old friend. I have never thought of Gavin as anything other than that, but right now we are both single adults and he is beautiful.

Dinner was nice and the conversation was easy. This feels familiar, but seems strange that Patrick and Stacy are not with us.

I found myself staring at Gavin throughout dinner. His mother is originally from Spain and his dad is American...he has the best of each. I feel I am memorizing each of his perfect features: Large full lips that smile easily over white teeth, olive skin that has recently been kissed by the sun, dark mussed up hair that screams for me to run my fingers through, and dark lashes and brows that does nothing but accentuate his heavenly blue eyes. He is stunning.

I watch his eyes change during dinner. One minute they are the softest most kind dark blue eyes, and then the next they are as mischievous as a little boy, but when he turns to me I feel them try to devour me.

Our plates are taken from the table, and we make plans to move over to Creegan's Irish Pub for drink. Gavin reaches over and laces his fingers in mine. He leans and whispers in Spanish "It feels strange to be out together without our spouses."

My eyes scan the room, and then reply in the same language. "I keep looking around for them to come back to the table." He unlaces my hand and holds it to his mouth and places a soft kiss. "But they won't."

He then rubs the inner part of my arm, and it sends shivers through my body. "The last time we all ate together it was a much bigger crowd." Referring to the people at our table.

Gavin replies, "Yes, to the tune of 8 couples crammed into your tiny house." I laugh and add, "You weren't complaining."

"I know...you were feeding me...there's no way I would turn down your cooking."

"Thank you."

"Ok stop. Us uni-lingual people are being left out," Garrett huffs, using made up words and incorrect grammar challenging me to correct him.

"Uni-lingual? Is that even a word?" I ask.

"Sorry, she needs to practice her Castilian Spanish before it's lost forever." So true. My college professor was originally from Madrid, and the Spanish I was taught is different from what is typically spoken in Arkansas. Most of the Spanish I hear comes from the Americas and even then not much.

Linda pulls me aside as we walk out of the restaurant. "I guess you don't need to take your pill after all?"

"No, I don't...and thank you for this. It has been nice, but I still can't believe you got me a date with Gavin." She smirks at me, "It was his idea."

Gavin immediately takes the position at my right side, and places his hand on my back. He's not quite as tall as the other men in my life, but it feels wonderful.

"We'll meet you there," Garrett calls to us as we leave Boscos. We agree.

Gavin leans in and whispers, "You look absolutely beautiful." I beam at his praise. "I feel like a very lucky man."

He walks me to the vehicle and opens the door like the gentleman I know he is. As he takes his place behind the wheel, he reaches over and laces his fingers in mine, and says, "I'm so glad you are here with me."

"So am I."

It is a short drive over the river to the pub, and we meet Garrett and Linda at the entrance. It is not as busy as I was expecting for a Saturday night, but it was still early. We make our way back to where an Irish band is playing, and find a seat.

We spend time catching up...talking about our adventures in California, our kids (Gavin doesn't have any), our jobs...everything. As the evening grows later, the pub becomes more crowded.

Our conversation lingers, and Gavin bends toward my ear and whispers, "I want to see you again." I nod my response, and he places his hand on my back underneath my hair and rubs my spine with his thumb. I close my eyes and sink into his warm touch.

"Do you know how wonderful I feel, knowing every man envies me right now?"

I laugh and shake my head, "You're funny."

His expression is not one of humor. "Seriously, look around. I am getting glared at. Take a look over there." He tilts his head toward the bar. I look past him and see Cooper, Foster and Michael with murderous looks toward my date.

"Don't worry about them. Those are my bodyguards. I thought I ditched them for the night...I guess not." He laughs and leans in to whisper again, "Don't look now, I think they are coming over."

I give him a weak smile, "I'm sorry."

"Don't be."

My three protectors make their way to our table. Michael is the first to extend a hand and meet Gavin. He gives Gavin the once over and tries to intimidate him...but he is unsuccessful. Foster leans over kisses my temple and dares Gavin to say anything about it. "You look gorgeous." I nod and say thank you, and then he offers his hand sizing up my date.

Cooper is the last to greet us. He places his hand on my back...skin on skin, and I almost catch on fire. "You are so beautiful," he says only loud enough for me to hear. My breath hitches...I feel his eyes burning through my skin.

I don't think he knows how much his touch affects me. I look at his face...blank, friendly, brotherly...Damn.

I put my hand on his arm and give it a few squeezes, and then introduce him to my date. He shakes Gavin's hand. He's cordial, almost friendly.

This is hard...It is hard to be just his friend.

Cooper's POV:

Beginning Friday night...

"What the hell were you thinking?" Will's voice booms through my living room.

I shake my head form side to side. "Don't start." I let Addy sleep over at Helen's house, and I've been drinking since I got home from work.

"You look like shit."

"Thanks."

Will sits down and gives me a sympathetic look.

Since Emily told me she had accepted a date with someone else, I have felt sick. I have been waiting for signs that she was no longer grieving for her husband, before I let her know how I feel. Now, I feel sick. How did I miss the signs?

I enjoy spending time with her. She was right when she said most of our time has been watching sports. I could kick my own ass for not taking into consideration that she would like to do something else. She always has been agreeable. I was having so much fun being with her, I didn't even think.

"Well, now it seems she's ready to get back out there. You might need to step up your game if you want her."

"I haven't even started my game." I take another drink. This whole thing sucks. How am I supposed to act happy for her, when she should be with me. "I take that back. This isn't a game." There I said it. It's not a game, or if it is I'm playing for keeps.

Will leaves after a few minutes, giving me time to wallow in self-pity.

Emily is perfect. She's beautiful, genuine, loving, with no false modesty, she loves Addy...perfect. Over the past few months, I have kept my feelings in check when I'm with her, giving me a chance to truly get to know her...and I love her.

After waking up early on Saturday, I head into work early. I want to do anything that would keep my mind off of the rock that landed in the pit of my stomach. I spent most of the night running 'what ifs' through my head. I hate this feeling...helpless. My only saving grace was that this is only one date.

Addy comes bopping into the house. I hear her yelling, "You got to see Ms. Cahill. She's beautiful." I smile at her and shake my head, "She's always beautiful."

"Not like this." The words are barely out of her mouth when Emily walks into the living room. She has the ability to take my breath away, but I have never seen her look like this. She smiles at me, and I know she can here me breathing.

I can't help the look of adoration that has crept onto my face. I want to pick her up, hold her, and tell her I love her. "Beautiful doesn't even come close to describing the way you look." She blushes. "Your hair...I just want to touch it. I've never seen it down. Amazing," I whisper for only her to hear. I can't stop my hands; I reach out and touch her hair. It's the first time I've seen it down. I want to see it splayed across my pillow.

Addy squeals, "Kiss her, you need to kiss her." Oh, hell yeah, I need to kiss her. I want to kiss her like she's mine, but I won't. This is Emily and I need to take it slow. I lean in watching her watch me. Her eyes move from my eyes to my lips and back again. Does she want me to kiss her? My breath hitches and so does hers. I press my lips into the corner of her mouth. Oh, god...I want more. I steady my breathing so I can move away.

I forgot Addy was in the room until I heard her squeal.

"Happy? I kissed her." And I would do it again in a heartbeat.

Addy picked up her shopping bags and said, "I'll leave you two alone now. My job here is done."

My hands move back to Emily's hair. I love the affect she has on me. "Beautiful is just not a good enough word to describe you." She stares into my eyes and then again to my lips. I affect her. "Thanks," is all she says.

Then, I take a step back and put my mask back on.

This evening has been a blur. What the hell am I going to do?

I can't tell you who won the game. My thoughts have been wrapped up in Emily. Will and Michael did what they could to keep me from feeling like such a dumb ass. Nothing has worked. I just hope she is having a miserable time, like I am.

We walk a few blocks to a bar to have a drink before calling it a night. As soon as I walk in, my heart sinks to the pit of my stomach. Emily is sitting at a table, looking even more beautiful than I have ever seen her. It knocks the air out of my lungs.

I stand and watch the interaction between her and that guy, trying to keep my emotions off of my face. She is completely engrossed in the conversation at her table. She doesn't look around like she is bored with his company. She's not looking for a distraction. She seems comfortable, happy.

I feel anger creep up in me. He plays with her hair and puts his hand on her back...and rubs. He keeps leaning in to whisper to her, and I watch, as she does not try to distance herself from him.

Michael and Will let me know that they see her. They show their concern.

She moves her head away from him and does a scan of the room with her eyes. I watch her lean in and whisper while he rubs her back. I can feel anger rising up in me more. They seem quite cozy for someone who has just met. I want to go over and rip his arm from his body.

I walk with Michael and Will to the table. I speak to Garrett and Linda listening while Emily introduces her date. Shit, they were already friends.

That won't stop me...I place my hand on her back and feel the electicity surge through me.

Please vote and or comment...I'll fix errors as soon as I can get time to edit. Thank you

Chapter 19 - Trying to Avoid the Issue

In every real man a child is hidden that wants to play. - Friedrich Nietzsche

Chapter 19 - Trying to Avoid the Issue

Emily's POV:

"Are you avoiding me?" Cooper startles me because I did not even hear him walk up. I've been working in the garden at Foster's house while Addy, Mason, Peyton, and Chandler swim.

"No, I've just been busy." I hope that my lie is not showing on my face. I've been trying to avoid him ever since my first date with Gavin. It was incredible how wonderful my night was until Cooper showed up. I was enjoying thinking of my friend as something more than friends, and then Cooper touched me. It took a lot of work on my part to remove him from my thoughts.

"Is this what it's going to be like? You start dating and you don't have time for your friends?" I've only seen him a few times in the last two weeks and each time short...on purpose, but I miss him.

"No, that's not how it is. I'm sorry."

With a quick smile he says, "Forgiven. Now how about going to dinner with me tonight."

I look away toward the children; I don't want to see his eyes. "I have plans already."

"With him?"

"Yes." This will be the fourth date with Gavin. Tonight will be the first time we are alone. Our first date was a double with Linda and Garrett. That ended with the softest sweetest goodnight kiss. It started as a chaste kiss on my lips, then as soft kiss to my upper lip then my lower lip, and then a lingering kiss that held promise for more.

We hiked Pinnacle Mountain on our second date with Mason, Edward, and my nephew Holden. We ended our day by playing Frisbee in the park. Somewhere along the way Mason decided to make it tackle Frisbee. Actually, just tackle mom Frisbee. Before I left Gavin gave me a small sweet kiss on the lips. Not quite as romantic as our first kisses because this time we had an audience, but I smiled all the way home.

Our third date was coffee as I waited for Peyton's doctor's appointment. Gavin works in emergency medicine at children's hospital, and he took a break to meet us. Peyton was certainly the center of attention for us. He was asking a million questions without a breath in between. Gavin remarked on how articulate he was, and how he has blossomed from the boy he met less than a year ago.

When he walked me to my car, he held open my door and reached up to touch my face. That one simple gesture sent a shiver through my body. He pulled me close and our mouths touched gently at first. The kiss was full of promise and longing. He pulled away from me, and watched my reaction. He must have liked what he saw because he came back for more, and then, he took charge of the kiss. His tongue swept my lips begging for entrance, which I freely gave. The kiss became passionate before I pulled away and rested my forehead to his. "Wow, that was nice." And my only response was "mmmm."

The worst part of our last date was that when I closed my eyes later and thought of our kiss, it wasn't Gavin's face I saw. It was Cooper's.

Cooper moves beside me as I pull the weeds from around the zucchini plants. So much for avoiding him. "Then let me help you so I can at least spend a little time with you." He kneels down beside me helping me weed.

"So, what is keeping you so busy?" He smiles at me in a way that makes me wish he wasn't just a friend. I shake the thought of my head and move on to staking tomato plants.

"Since school is out, I've been taking the kids to my parent's house to swim in the lake. Mason had soccer camp this past week, and I finally decided to tackle the last of the boxes in the garage." I try not to look at him, because it's hard not to want him. "How have you been?"

"Lonely...I miss you." Nothing more than just those four words...he misses me. His eyes were soft and it felt like they were caressing my face. "I've missed you, too."

I finish the garden, and even harvest some herbs for a yet to be determined purpose.

The heat is getting to me. It's time to cool off. "How long do you have before you head back to work?"

"I took the rest of the day off." I wonder what the occasion is, but I don't ask.

"Did you bring your suit?" I asked as I look over to watch the kids.

"I have one in the house." He leaves to change in his swimsuit.

"Momma, you gonna get wet?" Peyton asks as he is splashing in Chandler's arms. "We playin'. It's fun."

"I'll be right there." I strip off my shorts and shirt and put them on a table by the pool. I adjust my purple swimsuit. I was expecting to swim only with the children and I feel my suit is a bit revealing for me in mixed company. It looks more like a long v-neck sports bra with bikini bottoms.

Mason chuckles at me, and tells me I look fine, "Mom, really girls wear nothing more than strings sometimes."

"That may be true, but..." Looking down at my body making sure that all main parts can stay covered.

I hurry and rinse off to jump in before Cooper makes it outside.

"Oh my god, you've got to stop doing that." A husky voice said from behind me. I feel my face burn, thinking of what I look like with water pouring down my body. I look away trying to calm my embarrassment.

Cooper lifts my chin to look at him. "That's so cute." He uses his other hand to rub his thumb over my cheek.

"Stop, you're embarrassing me." I turn away from him quickly and jump in the pool. I look back and watch him as he enters. He looks like an Adonis with his light colored hair, blue eyes. He has wide toned chest; and he doesn't look like a weightlifter; he has a body of a runner. It's just not fair to look that good.

Peyton reaches for me as soon as I emerge from the water. "You gonna play?"

Before I can answer Mason dives under the water and grabs my legs trying to pull me under. Thank goodness Addy is there to defend me.

I chastise Mason for messing with me while Peyton is in my arms. We need to not scare Peyton and give him an unhealthy fear of water. Cooper agrees, and then comes to rescue Peyton from my arms. "Ok, Mason she's all yours."

"Thanks a lot. I thought you were my friend."

"I am but this is too much fun." He laughs in the most boyishly exuberant way. His eyes are bright and playful, and the sight of him takes my breath away. Fun, playful Cooper is a sight to behold.

Mason comes after me again, but this time I swim away and he goes past me. I'm able to jump on his back, which is a wrong move. He immediately heads to deeper water, taking me with him. When Mason reaches the bottom he flips me over his shoulder and rockets himself to the surface.

I swim away from him as fast as I can; splashing him with as much water as possible. Addy and Chandler join me with the splashing and it's three against one. Mason takes Chandler by the waist and dunks her, which makes her fight for control. She climbs on his back and grabs hold of his chest from behind and pushes him under.

Addy takes Peyton so she can rest for a minute, and Cooper swims up beside me. "Let's show these young pups a thing or two." I nod in agreement.

Cooper rises out of the water and uses his whole body to splash Mason. The move made a huge wave that returned and soaked him again. "No fair!" Mason yells.

Cooper laughs and raises his hand for me to high five. "Score."

"This is war." Chandler and Mason use their skills to push as much water as possible at Cooper and me.

I was beside Cooper but just a step or two in front, which made me the better target. Cooper puts his arm completely around my waist, and pulls me behind him. I cling to his back as he took the teenagers brutal attack, and when they were finished he moves me beside him to help with his attack. Defending myself from splashes is the only distraction I have to Cooper and his body.

This back and forth continues until the teens decide it's time for food. As the they leave I look over at Cooper, "It's nice to see you happy. Sometimes you are so serious, it's nice that you can let go."

His smile is infectious. "You make me happy," he beams at me.

Please vote and/or comment

Chapter 20 - Shut up and Kiss Me

P art of this chapter is repeated in two different points of view.

Kiss me and you will see how important I am. - Sylvia Plath

Chapter 20 - Shut up and kiss me.

Emily's POV:

The sun and water wore me out today and I'm paying for it in the form of a headache. Two doses of acetaminophen and it's just now beginning to ease.

Foster is in the living room with the kids. He missed out on the fun this afternoon, so he wanted to hang out with them and have a movie night. I think Cooper is coming over to join him later, but I'm not sure.

Twenty minutes to go, and I now have to rush. If I hadn't laid down for so long this wouldn't be a problem.

I slip on my bright teal sundress with a mock wrap front, and zip the side. The color of the dress brightens my face, so I no longer look as bad as I feel.

I pull my hair into a loose, messy bun. A little concealer under my eyes, gray shadow over, and a bit more mascara...now I look like I'm ready.

The doorbell rings followed by the voices of Foster and Gavin. When I enter the foyer, Foster moves into protector mode. He immediately wraps his arms around me, and narrows his eyes as he looks at Gavin. Then, he kisses my temple, "You look great. How are you feeling?" Gavin's expression changes to one of concern. I harden my look at Foster and his big mouth. "I'm feeling fine."

I look over to Gavin, "I had a headache. I'm fine now." Knowing that fine is never a good desciption for him. "Sorry, I know you don't like that word. I am medicated and on my way to a full recovery."

"You've become a doctor now?" He chuckles, but still looking concerned.

"No, I just figured you would understand more clinical speak. I just clarified my 'fine-ness'." I raise my eyebrows challenging either man to say anything. Foster's hand finds my shoulder, "You are always fine..."

"Not what I meant."

"True none the less." I let this conversation die, because I was ready to be on my way.

"So, where you kids off to?" Foster asks with a touch of humor.

"Dinner. Probably followed by a drink somewhere. Is that ok with you?" Gavin spoke directly to Foster.

"As long as she's back before her curfew."

I shake my head at both men.

"Shall we go?" Gavin asks as he takes my hand in his.

"Yes."

As we pull out of my neighborhood, "Honestly, how do you feel?" I could punch Foster and his big mouth.

"I feel better. I was a bit waterlogged from today, and probably a little dehydrated. I just had a headache. Honestly, I'm ok." He nods his head, "Good." His hand moves down my arm, and intertwines with my fingers.

This feels easy, nice, comfortable, and familiar, but it's not home. What's wrong with me? I long for someone that I can't have, and I feel nothing but friendship for one that could be more. I tell my brain to shut up...keep an open mind.

Gavin puts his hand on my back as we walk into the restaurant. His touch is light, soft and comforting. He holds open the door, and his eyes are warm and inviting when they meet mine. I still cannot believe such a beautiful man is with me. I push back my earlier thoughts and concentrate on the man before me.

I hear our waitress catch her breath when she caught a full view of Gavin. She openly stares at him while taking our order. As she leaves the table, I look over to my date who is completely oblivious of the young lady's admiration. "Does that happen everywhere you go?"

"What?" Gavin asks completely sincere.

I watch our retreating waitress. "She was completely enamored with your looks." He shakes his head. "What would happen if she actually knew your heart?"

He meets my eyes, and he has a little bit a devious smile. "Do you know my heart?"

I shake my head. "Only the part you've shown me so far. I've seen it when you're with my children. I've seen it when you were my neighbor. I've seen it with Stacy." With her name I see sadness flash in his eyes barely long enough to register, but it is there.

"I'm sorry. I didn't mean to cause you pain."

"You didn't, not really." He looks away then after a moment he asks, "Can I ask you something?"

"Yes," I smile at him. "Anything."

"When does it start getting easier?"

"I was hoping you could tell me. You're farther along than me when it comes to our loss. Stacy's been gone..."

Before I could even finish my sentence, "One year, two months, and sixteen days." I look at him in shock. I sometimes literally have to think back and count to remember how long it has been since Patrick was killed. Even though it's been almost nine months. Sometimes it feels so long ago. I would have to calculate how many weeks or days, but I feel like its getting better...like I'm ready to move on.

My life has changed a lot from what it was. I was a mother and wife, and now I have to be a mother and father. I have to be strong for my boys and I have a phenomenal amount of support.

"I miss her every single day." And there it is, I just got moved from a possible future 'something' to 'friend.' So, I accept my role and hold his hand while he talks about his dead wife.

We spend the rest of dinner talking about our spouses, and life without them. And while the talk I realize that I'm no longer mourning Patrick, or at least not in the same way Gavin is mourning Stacy. I miss him, but Patrick would be pissed that I was not moving on with my life. He would want me to be happy. His love was strong and he would want me to love again. That thought should make me a little sad, but it doesn't - it makes me smile.

After dinner we stroll down by the riverfront, enjoying each other's company. The atmosphere between us has changed now. Even though I did not feel that we had a lot of chemistry, I liked the idea that there was the possibility. Now I have another 'just friend' to add to my stack. I should be happy. I like having friends, but the idea of 'just friends' makes my stomach tighten. What's wrong with me that I'm always going to be everybody's 'just friend'?

Gavin drives me home and our conversation stays on neutral ground, none of the previous emotional topics are brought back up. He walks me to the front door, and kisses me sweetly on the lips. Even though he hasn't said anything, this kiss screams friendship. It is no longer the promising kisses we shared before...chaste friendship...nothing more.

I put my purse down on the table by my front door, and Foster yells to let me know he is in the living room. "Where are the kids?" I ask as I make my way into the room.

"Peyton and Mason have gone to bed, and I put the girls in the guest room. They were tired, and I didn't want to leave until I could talk to you. Is that ok?" Foster turns off the television before he even turnes to look at me.

"That's fine." Foster's expression changes when he finally looks at me.

"Now, tell me what's wrong."

"I think something is wrong with me."

"Your head? Are you ok?" I chuckle.

"No, headache is gone. But I think something is wrong with me." I begin to cry into his chest. Not the sweet tears that can be brushed away with a thumb, but big ugly sobs. Foster wraps his arms around me, and lets me sink into his comfort and cry.

"What did he do?" I heard him whisper in my hair. I shake my head to let him know Gavin didn't do anything. "Do I need to hurt him?"

I chuckle through my tears, "No, he didn't do anything. He's a friend...just a friend."

"You don't sound so happy about that."

"It's fine. I didn't feel much more than friendship for him anyway. But, what is wrong with me that every man I know just wants to be my friend? Am I that broken?"

"You are far from broken." He pulls me into a deeper hug, and holds me. My head starts to hurt again. Not like earlier, this time it's from the tears, and the emotions.

"I sometimes wish..." I don't finish my sentence, because it doesn't matter what I wish.

"Tell me."

"Cooper," is all I say.

"I'm going to let you go, I'll see you in the morning." I look up at him in shock, and he kisses my forehead.

"I think you two need to talk." He barely gets the words out of his mouth and I feel a hand on my shoulder.

Cooper's POV:

I couldn't have asked for a more perfect day. I finally caught up with Emily, and let her know that I missed her. We spent hours in the pool playing with the kids. It felt like family...it felt like home.

She is absolutely a breath of fresh air. She has never acted like she is too old to play with the kids, but when she talks with me I always feel like I have her undivided attention. I don't know of anyone she doesn't make feel special. Maybe it's because she is special...I sound like a girl.

I should have gone back to work this afternoon, but after seeing her for the first time in days, there was no way I was going to say goodbye. We swam with the kids until we were utterly exhausted, and it was one of the best days of my life...until she left and the knowledge she was going out with him again. I want to wrap her up in my arms and tell her exactly how I feel. But I don't.

I spend the evening with the kids again watching movies at Emily's house with Will. I didn't want to sit around the house by myself. I didn't trust my thoughts...I didn't want them to dwell on Emily.

Will and I wanted to wait for Emily to come home from her date. He wants to talk to her. I just figured Gavin wouldn't stay around if Emily had us in the house.

I check on Peyton and the girls, and as I am on my way back to the living room, I hear Emily crying. The first thing I feel is anger. What happened to make Emily cry? It had to bad. She is one of the strongest people I've ever met.

"What did he do?" I feel my fists tightened, waiting for the answer. She doesn't say anything.

"Do I need to hurt him?" No, Will that is my job.

"No, he didn't do anything. He's a friend...just a friend." My heart beats faster...friend. I feel the smile forming on my face, and then it falls. She's upset they are friends. She wanted more?

"You don't sound so happy about that." Putting my hand on the wall and dropping my head, I hold my breath waiting for the answer. I know I need to let her know I'm here, and give her a hug...but I just wait.

"It's fine. I didn't feel much more than friendship for him anyway. But, what is wrong with me that every man I know just wants to be my friend? Am I that broken?" I find it hard to swallow. She doesn't have feelings for him. Now my smile is back.

"You are far from broken." Not broken at all. In fact you are perfect.

"I sometimes wish..."

"Tell me." I wait to see if she finishes her thought, but she doesn't. I take a few steps into the room, so she knows I'm here for her.

"Cooper," What? Was that her answer, or does she see me?

"I'm going to let you go, I'll see you in the morning." Will kisses her, and then nods to me to come speak to her. I walk over and touch her shoulder.

"I think you two need to talk." With that Will leaves Emily's house.

She looks at me with her face still not completely recovered from her sobs. "How long have you been here?"

"A long time." I reach down and wipe her face. Every emotion I feel about this woman is written on my face. I am holding nothing back. I don't want to scare her, but she needs to know how I feel.

She looks away from me...embarrassed. "Oh."

"Tell me what's wrong? Look at me, and tell me what's wrong." She stares at my face like she does so often. She looks at my eyes, then down to my lips, then back to my eyes. She's trying to read me.

"I'm just feeling sorry for myself." She gives me a weak smile, and I move my hand down her arm to hold her hand. I find that when I hold her hand, she talks to me more openly. Or at least she usually does. "It seems that I make great friend material."

"Without a doubt that is true." She blows out a breath and her chin waivers. I reach down and lift her chin. "You are a great friend."

"Thanks," she says puts her head in my chest.

"Can I tell you a story?" I blow out a breath, knowing it is too late to retract my words...now or never.

"Sure," she doesn't sound very happy.

"The first time I saw you, I felt like I had to fight for air. You completely took my breath away. I was so pissed at Will for meeting you first. I wanted to kill him. I've never had a reaction to a woman quite like I had when I met you." She doesn't say anything, or even move.

I continue, "Then, Michael was there, and then Mason and Peyton...I was trying to understand what was going on, but what I really wanted to know was who did I have to get rid of to make you look at me." I laugh remembering how it felt the first time I met her. "And then, you started becoming my friend. I couldn't wait to start my day with you. Meeting you for a morning run was the best part of my day. I love you as my friend. I hoped for more, and I thought we were headed there until the night you told me about Patrick." I groaned bracing myself for the most frustrating memory.

"That very next morning, I had decided I would be your 'friend only' while you grieve. We sat out on your deck and it was the first time truly felt at peace since my sister died." I feel her shift, but she makes no sounds.

"I wanted to be there for you, like it felt like you were for me. But that changed quickly. The peace I felt with was gone in a heart beat." I hear her crying. I lean back so I can see her face. "There is a lot more to this story. Just listen." I am pleading with her.

"Having Will walk into your kitchen after we had spent such a nice morning together, pissed me off more that I could put into words. I was livid. I thought you had gotten drunk and slept with Will." I reach down and clean her face again. Our eyes meet. "It was wrong. I was so wrong. I am so sorry." I kiss her forehead, and hold my lips on her.

"You were, I mean are very feisty. You didn't let me get away with it. You told me to figure out what I wanted...friendship or not. The way you put it, there was only two options. Friend...with you in my life, or...not friend...with you not in my life. I knew at that moment that 'not friend' was not an option." I move my hands down her back soothing her, and letting her know where this story will end.

"I have tried to be your friend ever since you returned from Europe, and I have loved every single moment. I was willing to be your friend forever, but not anymore. I can't be your friend." Emily gasps and tries to catch her breath. I move away so our eyes meet, again. I need to help her stay calm. "I can't be 'only' your friend anymore. My feelings have changed."

She looks at me confused by my words, maybe processing everything that has been said. She studies my face all over again.

"I don't understand."

"I like you for so much more than friends. And I need to know if you feel anything for me." There isn't a sound from Emily...she's just staring.

"Emily say something. I've just given you the power to hurt me, but I don't want you to."

"I won't hurt you." She smiles at me, and her chin quivers. I reach down and stop her chin. I press my lips gently to hers, hoping her words means that she is willing to give me a chance.

Her lips are soft and hesitate as ours meet, and then she moves closer. My hands immediately move to her face and I caress her as I gain entrance to her mouth. I tentatively stoke her tongue with mine, and hers joins in what feels like a slow erotic dance. I explore her mouth pulling her closer. Before we get ahead of ourselves, I pull back putting my forehead on hers. "I've been waiting a long time to do that."

A tear escapes down her cheek as she looks up at me. "Me, too."

Inspiration struck and I did not even go back to check for errors. I will edit soon.

Please vote and/or comment. I truly enjoy hearing from you.

Thanks.

Chapter 21 - Where do We Go From Here

This chapter is repetitive since it contains Emily's POV of the same scene from Chapter 20.

My belief is that communication is the best way to create strong relationships. - Jada Pinkett Smith

Chapter 21 - Where do We Go From Here

Emily's POV:

"It seems that I make great friend material." I tell Cooper hoping he could cheer me up, but I doubt that he can today.

"Without a doubt that is true." I exhale the breath I didn't know I was holding, and then Cooper lifts my chin to look at him chin. "You are a great friend."

"Thanks," I say. He's over 6 feet tall and I'm not even as tall as his shoulders. I lean foreword and I bury my forehead against his chest, hiding my face from him.

"Can I tell you a story?" He blows out a breath. He must be trying to come up with a way to explain how being friends is so much better than anything else.

"Sure," is my only response.

"The first time I saw you, I felt like I had to fight for air. You completely took my breath away. I was so pissed at Will for meeting you first. I wanted to kill him. I've never had a reaction to a woman quite like I had when I met you." He takes a breath.

He continues, "Then, Michael was there, and then Mason and Peyton...I was trying to understand what was going on, but I really wanted to know was who did I have to get rid of to make you look at me. And then, you started becoming my friend." That's how he felt. I thought he hated me. "I couldn't wait to start my day with you. Meeting you for a morning run was the best part of my day. I love you as my friend. I hoped for more, and I thought we were headed there when you told me about Patrick." He groans and I hold my breath remembering...

"That very next morning, I had decided I would be your 'friend only' while you grieve. We sat out on your deck and it was the first time I truly felt at peace since my sister died." Peace that is what I feel when I'm with him.

"I wanted to be there for you, like it felt like you were for me. But that changed quickly. The peace I felt with was gone in a heart beat." His words rip through me. He doesn't feel the same anymore. "There is a lot more to this story. Just listen." His words soothe me.

"Having Will walk into your kitchen after we had spent such a nice morning together, pissed me off more that I could put into words. I was livid. I thought you had gotten drunk and slept with Will." He moves me away from him and lifts my chin so that see his eyes. "It was wrong...I was wrong...I am so sorry." He kisses my forehead and keeps his lips on me. Cooper doesn't do that...that's a classic Foster move.

"You were, I mean are very feisty. You didn't let me get away with it. You told me to figure out what I wanted...friendship or not. The way you put it, there was only two options: 1. friend - with you in my life, or 2. not friend - with you not in my life. I knew at that moment that 'not friend' was not an option."

"I have tried to be your friend ever since you returned from Europe, and I have loved every single moment. I was willing to be your friend forever, but not anymore. I can't be your friend." Oh god, he doesn't even want to be friends. My eyes are stinging...I can't breathe...breathe...breathe.

He moves so he is looking in my eyes. I have to get out of here. I can't do this. I can't breathe. "I can't be only your friend anymore. My feelings have changed."

What? I look at his face. I'm not sure what he is thinking. He looks very sweet, but his words sound like goodbye. Is he saying goodbye? "I don't understand."

"I like you for so much more than friends. And I need to know if you feel anything for me." My heart is racing. It's pounding out of my chest. He likes me. This 'whatever it is' isn't one sided?

"Emily, say something." I let out a breath. "I've just given you the power to hurt me, but I don't want you to."

My eyes widen at his words. "I won't hurt you." I would never want to hurt you. I feel my chin begin to quiver...I think I'm about to cry.

He pulls my chin up, and his lips find mine. His kiss is soft and firm, but I want more. I tilt my head to deepen the kiss, and he touches my face as my tongue meets his. Electricity explodes and runs through my body as he slowly kisses and explores my mouth. He pulls me closer, and firmly holds me to his chest. Before I have a chance to touch him, he pulls back and rests his forehead to mine. "I've been waiting a long time to do that," he says.

"Me, too." I feel a tear, and then his thumb run across my cheek.

As much as my body wants to jump up into his arms and hold him, my mind is staring at him in shock. I want to get as close to him as possible, but I also want to pull away and look at his handsome face. I am so confused at this very moment. Everything I thought I knew about him has changed in the most amazing way, and my heart is soaring.

I want to feel him; I want to know him in this new way. I have barely dared touch him before, but with his words it's like he gave me permission. As if my hands have a mind of their own, they reach for Cooper's hands.

"I want to touch you." He nods his permission and leans against the arm of my couch. I watch his face as my hands begin to memorize him. I touch the back of his hands rubbing my thumbs over his knuckles, before they circle around to his palms and intertwine his fingers. I smile at him because I am touching him knowing this is not friendly...this is a beginning.

I move my hands so that his fingers are touching the backs of my hands. Then, my fingers trace the muscles of his forearm up and back down. As my hands continue to travel to his biceps, I smile at Cooper. These are the arms I have longed to touch and hold, and now I am.

He is being very patient as I explore. He is watching me. My hands travel to the front part of his shoulders up to his neck. I trace his jaw with my thumbs and hear his breath hitch. I gently pull his face to mine and kiss him.

But this one, this one is my kiss. I tilt my head to the side and take his top lip between mine, and then move to his bottom lip grazing it with my teeth. As our tongues meet I feel my body begin to burn. He holds me close to him, one hand at the back of my neck, the other around my waist. He takes over the kiss and sets my body on fire.

My hands are busy exploring his face, neck, and hair; and he just holds me firmly to himself.

He traces my jaw with his lips until he finds my neck. The heat I felt intensifies, and he takes my breath away. He lets a moan, and my body immediately sinks closer to him.... home.

The thought scares me back into reality, and I pull away from Cooper. When our eyes meet, I see his full of desire and lust. I put my forehead to his and steady my breathing. My hands continue their exploration of his shoulders, tracing his collarbone with my fingers. "May I?" He nods, and I unbutton the first few buttons of his shirt, and place my hand in the center of his chest. I feel his rapid heart beat through my fingertips.

He stands in front of me, and I lean in putting my cheek over his heart. I listen to his heartbeat, and feel my heart speed up to keep tempo with his.

"So, where do we go from here?" I ask.

"That's up to you."

"Then, I want to stay like this for a while." He pulls me closer and holds me. I sink into the comfort of his arms, holding him cherishing this moment for as long as it lasts.

"Come, let's sit down," Cooper whispers and moves me over to the couch.

Even though I miss his touch, I choose to sit away from him. His eyes sparkle as he looks at me. There are so many questions running through my mind, "Why didn't you ever tell me this before?"
Cooper gives me a weak smile, "I thought it was one-sided, and then when I found out about Patrick...I wasn't going to chase after a grieving widow.

I have been waiting for you. Waiting for you to be ready for me to tell you how I feel." Watching him talk, I can see he is laying all out on the table. I'm not sure how deep his affection goes, but I see that this is different than what I had thought.

"How long?" He smiles at my question.

"How long have I been waiting, or how long have I felt this way?"

"Both," I ask, staring into his eyes watching his face as he answers.

"I have felt this way from the moment I first saw you - it's just grown from there. I've been waiting since you came back from Europe."

I move closer to give him a slow tender kiss as his lips nibbles mine. Cooper holds my face in his hand, as his patient sensual kiss becomes one full of passion. His hands travel to the nape of neck as his lips move away from mine. His kisses a searing path along my jaw to my neck. Completely igniting a long forgotten sensation through my core. A small groan escaped from his throat, and he pulls back to steady his breathing.

"I've never been accused of being a patient man, but it's different with you." He reaches up and puts the palm of his hand on my cheek, and I lean into his touch. "I haven't minded the wait. It has given me a chance to get to know you...and again I've loved every minute of it."

"Now, I'm going to ask you a question from earlier. Where do we go from here?" I can't miss the desire in his eyes, but I can tell the question is not sexual.

"I'm not sure. I want to say let's play it by..." He puts his finger on my mouth before I can say 'ear.'

"Don't. I don't want to play this by ear. I've been doing that for a long time...just waiting for you. I want to make plans. I want to spend time with you away from a crowd. I want to spend as much time together as possible." He looks at me with expression somewhere between pleading and demanding. "I want you."

He bends his head, leans in, and nibbles on my lips. "Do you have plans for next Saturday?" He wants to wait a whole week to take me on a date? "Remove that thought from your head." He pulls back and kisses my forehead. "I intend to see you as much as you will let me this week, but Saturday I want you all to myself."

My heart skips a beat, and then begins to race. I cannot stop the smile from spreading across my face. "I'd love to spend Saturday with you.

"Then it's a date." He moves off the couch and checks the time. "It's late. You need some sleep." He pulls me up into his arms and rests his chin on my head.

I walk him to the back door for him to walk to his house. He bends down to kiss me goodnight. "I'm so glad we had this talk." His smile is completely infectious.

"I will see you," kiss "tomorrow," kiss "morning," kiss "early." He tells me with kisses emphasizing his words.

"Ok."

His hand was on the door, but he turns back around toward me. He picks me up to meet his lips. Lifting me off the ground, he crashes into my lips with more passion and heat than any of our previous kisses. His mouth is hungry and demanding. His hands are exploring the length of my back, pulling me closer to him. I hear a quick intake of air as his breathing increases. I let him guide me through his onslaught of lips and tongue. Not the gentle, soft, heated kisses from earlier. These kisses are primal, and I wrap my arms around his body holding on, giving as much as I'm taking.

As our kisses become slow he puts me down, kisses me gently on the forehead, whispers goodnight, and leaves.

Cooper's POV:

The sun is barely up, and I'm on Emily's deck knocking at her back door.

She comes to the door dressed in her running shorts and t-shirt, but with bare feet. The smile that is plastered on her face mirrors mine. "Good morning," she chokes out as I engulf her in my arms.

"I couldn't wait to see you," I tell her as I touch her face. She presses her cheek into my palm, and I lean in to kiss her. Hmmm is her only response. "Are you almost ready to hit the track?"

"Yes, let me get my shoes."

As we finish our first lap, I ask, "What time does all the excitement start today?" I think my question throws her off guard.

"Oh my god, I forgot." Today is cooking lessons for the girls.

"It's ok, they'll understand." I tell her and she puts her hand on my arms and squeezes a few times.

"It's not that," she bites her lip and looks pensive. "Gavin is coming. He is helping make paella, while I make tapas with the girls."

"What is it that worries you?" I have ten other questions, but I decide to start with this one.

"I don't know. I know I need to talk to him. He needs to know what happened."

"Do you have feelings for him?" I smile as I ask this question, trying not to look angry.

"Not really anything more than friendship, but I was open to explore the idea of more."

The next question shows my insecurity, but I have to know. "How do you feel about me?"

She looks me in the eyes, and her expression softens. "I'm not sure, yet, but it's already more...more than friends." I let out a breath I didn't know I was holding. I hug her tightly as a smile spreads across my face.

We walk back to my house holding hands. "I'm going to take a quick shower. I meet you back at your house and help you with breakfast for the kids." Our lips meet for a quick goodbye, and I watch her as she makes her way to the path that leads to her house.

"It's about damn time." Will says as soon as Emily leaves the table. He laughs at me when I glare. "I see everything worked out in your favor last night." Smiling I nod at him.

"So, what's going on?" He wants to know.

"We haven't gotten far enough to define it, but she is willing to see where this will lead."

"Where will this lead?" I shake my head like I don't know, but I know exactly where I want this to go.

Will doesn't stay very long after breakfast. He only came by to bring Chandler a change of clothes, and he will return for dinner.

It's almost three, and the kitchen is busy. I've already gotten 'knowing' looks from Ms. Hannah and Keira. Emily has the girls reading through their recipes, pulling out the ingredients needed, and preparing a their work surface. I doubt they have even had a chance to approach Emily, yet.

When the doorbell rings, I answer. "Gavin, nice to see you again." Keeping my face neutral will be a challenge, but for Emily I will try. "The ladies are all in the kitchen waiting for you."

"Thank you." I show him to the kitchen and find a place at the breakfast counter with Jim (Emily's dad) to watch the excitement...keep an eye of Gavin.

Gavin is introduced to everyone, and goes about preparing the paella. He talks to the girls about his grandmother's house in Spain, and about swimming in the Mediterranean Sea, while showing them how to make paella.

CJ and I help Gavin put the paella pan on the open grill. Emily joins us on the deck. She smiles brightly, and turns to Gavin and speaks in Spanish. "Where do you see this..." She motions between the two of them. "going?" Her Spanish is good, but she speaks slow enough for me to understand. She smiles and our eyes meet, and then her face drops. Gavin takes her elbow in his hand. His Spanish is much more fluent and I don't understand what he says, but Emily does. Her voice becomes softer and their conversation continues in whispers. I can feel my anger begin to consume me. Since I can't hear their conversation, I have to rely on body language to understand.

After a few minutes of trying to discern their conversation, I quit. I excuse myself from CJ and Jim and leave the house. I stay gone for over an hour, and when I return Emily comes over and squeezes my hand, and asks if I was ok. I didn't answer, because I am trying to remain calm. She nods and walks off.

When the food is ready Ms. Hannah plays host, and Emily is nowhere to be seen...neither was Gavin. He returned a few minutes after with a big smile on his face, but Emily was still missing. Anger burns as it reaches my face.

"Where is Emily?" Ms. Hannah thought she had gone to her room.

I knock, not exactly sure what I was doing there. There was no sound, so I knock again. I hear a muffled sound and open the door. "What are you doing?" Her hair is down, she was laying in the dark, and I could tell she was crying.

"I'm sorry," she says in a weak voice. I'm angry about her secret conversation with Gavin, is that why she is sorry? Or is because she chose Gavin? I don't say anything, because I don't trust myself to stay calm.

Jim comes in the room. "Your mom sent me in with this for you." He hands her a glass of water, and a medicine bottle. "How many do you need?"

"Two."

"What's wrong?" I ask, knowing whatever it is I probably caused it.

"Migraine," Jim says. "Stress triggered," and he stares at his daughter daring her to deny it. "She needs to rest for a while. Come on, let's go back."

"No, Cooper, stay." With that, Jim leaves the room.

I'm standing near the door, not wanting to move closer, yet. "Do these happen often?"

"No." She takes a deep breath. "Are you still mad at me?"

"Should I be?"

"I don't know." She shuts her eyes, and rolls away from me. "I don't know what I did, but I'm sorry it made you mad." I hear a soft groan leave her throat, and she is in a lot of pain.

Closing the gap between us, "When did this start?"

"Yesterday."

"You've had a migraine since yesterday?"

"No, I got the first headache yesterday." She whimpers. "It didn't really go away...now it's a migraine." She told me as I rub the back of her neck.

"What can I do for you?"

"Just hold me for a few minutes." She is silent and I think she has fallen asleep when I hear, "Why did you leave?"

"I didn't. I'm still here." I continue to sooth her head as we talk.

"No, earlier. Why did you leave?" Because I was jealous...happy.

"Tell me what happened with Gavin?"

She let out a deep breath. "I asked him what he thought there was between us. I needed him to tell me how he felt, so I would know how to approach the subject of you. He thinks of us as friends and maybe with benefits. So, it was pretty easy to tell him that I was dating you. He was happy for me. We are dating, right?" For the first time in a few hours, I felt myself relax.

"Yeah, we're dating." I run my hand down her back, and pull her closer to me.

I come clean to her, "I was mad earlier, but I think it was because I was scared. I see how the two of you are together, and I thought maybe you would rather be with him. Maybe you were choosing him. Even though I know what you said about him, the way you are so comfortable together, I was still a little worried."

She put her arm around my waist. "I told you I wouldn't hurt you. I meant it." I really hope so.

I lay on her bed with my head on her headboard, and pull her onto my chest. Her body relaxes and she falls asleep with my hands running through her hair.

———————————

Please vote and/or comment.

Chapter 22 - I Don't Want This

Warning: This chapter contains sexual content. It is not written to offend or meant to be explicit. Hopefully affection has been expressed in good taste.

Love involves a peculiar unfathomable combination of understanding and misunderstanding. - Diane Arbus

Chapter 22 - I Don't Want This

Cooper's POV:

Her hair has fallen to one side, as I rub her neck gently massaging the knots in her muscles. This is where I want to be...holding Emily. I need to remember that.

My hand continues to sooth her head, and this gentle act calms me. I am no longer mad or scared or even jealous. She is my solace, and I've known that for a while now. "I love you," I whisper in her hair.

I hear a soft knock on the door and it opens slowly. "How's she doing?" Jim asks.

"She's asleep."

"Good. Sometimes that works best." He looks at his daughter resting on my chest, and I can tell he wants to talk to me. I move Emily over to her pillow and follow Jim out of the room.

Everyone has gone home except for Jim and Ms. Hannah, and of course Addy. "We're going to take the boys home with us. Mason was wondering if Addy could come, also."

"She would like that. Thank you." Addy is all smiles and runs off to find Mason.

Jim walks into the kitchen and pulls out a small box filled with medication. "The medicine I gave Emily will probably leave her a little hung over when she wakes up." He pulls a bottle out and puts it on the counter. "If she needs more." He taps the bottle and leaves it beside the box.

"Why didn't she tell me she was in pain?"

"She's not a complainer. She takes that after her mom. Knowing her, she thought she would be ok." I shake my head at his words. "Don't feel bad. I didn't see it either, but Hannah did." Jim sat down next to me. "You know she's going to be mad at herself tomorrow."

"Why?"

"She had a house full of people, and she wasn't able to stay and entertain." He's right. She will be upset.

"She says this doesn't happen often."

"No, I know she had one a few months ago. Michael happened to stop by for something, and ended up staying the night." Jim gives me a curious look. "Like I said she's not much of a complainer. She also isn't forth coming with information that will cause someone to worry."

Out of all the months I've known her, the only time I've heard her complain was about not going to watch the Travelers play ball.

"So, how long have you been in love with my daughter?" I choke at the forwardness of his question.

"Son, it's as plain as the nose on your face. If I hadn't already guessed it months ago, what I just walked in on proves it." I smile at him, and he slaps my back. "Now let's talk about your temper."

Shit.

"Actually, I want to commend you. You took it better than most men I know. Most men would have pulled that doctor friend of hers to the side and punched him." I know my face is not hiding the shock I feel. "It's never easy seeing the woman you care about having an intimate conversation with another man."

"It's not easy. I almost lost it. I left to cool off instead."

"Wise choice." He says with a smile.

"My daughter is very special. In a family full of boys, she is a blessing." I nod in agreement. "She's been through a lot this past year, and I don't want to see her hurt again." I don't respond, because he is just being a protective father right now.

We sit in silence for a few minutes until Ms. Hannah and the kids came in carrying a suitcase. We say goodnight, and they are off to pack some clothes for Addy.

At the door of Emily's room, I stop and listen to her breathing. The rhythm is soft, slow and deep. She is resting. I lean over and kiss her softly on the cheek and lips, and then take a moment to admire the beauty that has now captured my heart.

The saying goes: If you always do what you've always done, you'll get what you've always gotten. Not this time. This time I want Emily, and this time I want forever. I will no longer rush the physical and ignore the emotional...I want them both.

Closing the door behind me, I make my way to the guest room to get some sleep.

Emily's POV:

The house is dark and completely silent. I reach over hoping to find Cooper, but I'm alone. The clock on the nightstand announces the time 2:48. "Ugghh," my head is still achy, but the nausea and stabbing pain is gone.

Stumbling out of bed, I head to Peyton's room to check on him. I know my parents or Mason has taken care of Peyton while I was out, but he's not in his bed, I smile to myself anticipating finding Mason and Peyton camped out together upstairs.

I turn the light on in the hallway and open Mason's bedroom door...they are not there. 'Surely they're not sleeping in the basement...it's not even finished, yet.'

I make my way down to the basement, looking in the different rooms. They are not there. I feel the rush of panic beginning to overtake me...breathe. I head upstairs and down the hallway to the guest room, hoping they decided to sleep in there.

"Cooper?" He rolls over.

"Are you ok?" He asks and sits up in bed.

"I can't find my boys." I know my voice sounds panicky, but that is exactly how I feel.

"Your parents took them home with them." A flood of relief waves through my body...my boys are ok.

"Why are you here?" I ask Cooper.

"I was worried about you. I didn't want you to be alone, in case you needed help."

"Thanks." I reach over and touch his arm, and I immediately want to be in them. I move the blanket so I can join him.

"Emily, stop." My hear sink to my stomach. I straighten the blanket back, and move toward the door.

"Wait. Please don't go." I turn back to him and hesitate but only for a moment. I'm not in my right mind, and I cannot handle a rejection right now. "Let me put on my pants." He moves off the bed and I catch a glance of his glorious backside, and my body reacts to the nude form before me.

"Oh."

He quickly puts his pants on, and he takes a few steps and engulfs me in his strong arms. "I'm sorry. I didn't want to make you nervous or uncomfortable finding me naked. Would you like to come lay down now?" I nod and he walks me back to the bed.

"Thank you for earlier." He began touching my hair, running his fingers through. His touch is soft and soothing, and I wonder if this is how he will always make me feel.

"Your muscles are still full of knots."

"I know. My dad told you my headache came from stress, but really more from tension. For the first time in a long while, I'm not stressed." I squeeze him to try to let him know that he is the reason. "I just have to learn how to relax my muscles so I don't trigger a migraine."

He chuckles, "Is this your way of guilting me into giving you a neck rub?"

"Is it working?" I smile and his hands move from soft and soothing to deep and kneading. Within minutes I am nothing but boneless mush. He has magic fingers...I blush as that idea fully registers.

I groan as he works out all the tension stored in my neck and shoulders. "This feels sooo good." He bends forward and kisses the back of my head. "I'm glad you like it."

His hands turn to soft and soothing again, and I'm more relaxed than I have been in a very long time. I roll over and he lies down beside me. "How do you feel?"

"Completely relaxed, thank you." He leans over and kisses my softly.

"Any time." Since Cooper told me of his feelings, I have taken time to think of all of our time together. Other than the unreadable expressions, he has shown me nothing but kindness and tenderness.

I settle in on his chest, my cheek over his heart. As his fingers play with my hair, I hear his heart rate increase. I place a kiss in the center of his bare chest, and work my way up to his neck. He makes small noises that urge me to continue.

I move on top of him and straddle his waist. I can feel how my body affects him, and he runs his hands up my body to my face and holds me. "My beautiful, beautiful Emily." His lips find mine and I trace his lips with my tongue. My body melts into his in sheer pleasure of unhurried affection.

His touch begins to burn me as his hands find the hem of my shirt. His fingers on my hips, he begins to explore my body setting me on fire. His fingers graze the skin under my breasts but settle on my ribs. With his thumbs on my ribs and his fingers on my back, he pulls me into a kiss forcing my mouth open. As the kisses become more heated and hurried, our breaths become more ragged.

In one swift movement he has me on my back, and he settles between my legs. The warmth of his body hovering over mine makes me loose all coherent thought. His kiss is insistent and demanding, and I am completely powerless...More.

I tighten my hold on him, pulling him even closer to my body. His mouth leaves mine and travels to my jaw, and then my neck. I hear myself cry out as he sets my body on fire with every touch of his hands and mouth. He pulls my top off of my shoulder exposing my breast. He nibbles and kisses as his tongue traces a heated path to my nipple. "Yes." I hear myself say.

He places soft kisses on my nipple before circling it with his tongue. Every part of my body is on fire for this man. He reaches down to the hem of my shirt and gently pulls it over my head. Skin on skin...burning.

My hands travel and explore this incredible sexy man, that has ignited what I had thought was dead and gone. I feel him stiffen above me, and my hands travel down his back to his waistband...More.

My hands trace his waist to the front and begin to undo his button. He lets out a moan, and I continue.

"Stop. I don't want this." His words are like a bucket of cold water. I try to swallow, but can't. I stiffen, and move him away from me, grab my shirt, and get out of bed.

Breathe...breathe.

I can't believe I was so stupid. I reach the door and try to open it before tears run down my face. What did I miss?

Chapter 23 - Let the Courtship Begin

This chapter is repetitive since it contains Cooper's POV of the incident that led to Emily leaving.

Passion momentary; love enduring - John Wooden

Chapter 23 - Let the Courtship Begin

Cooper's POV:

Emily springs up and bolts out the door before I can get off the bed. 'What the hell just happened?'

She rests her head on the center of my chest, and I wonder if she knows how comforting this feeling is. My hand runs through her hair, and I am content to just bathe in her warmth. Peace...I found peace. As much as my body wants her I am happy with just this.

Her lips plant soft, warm kisses over my heart, and begins to travel up my body. 'Hmmmm.' It takes less than a moment for my body to react to her.

Her leg moves over me, and from where she sits she should have no doubt about what her body does to mine.

She feels so good, and looks..."My beautiful, beautiful Emily," I say as I hold her face in my hands. I pull her to my lips and kiss her slowly and deeply, unrushed because we can have forever.

I touch her skin, running my fingers under her tank top...no bra. I smile. Caressing her hips, her back, her ribs...she is small. I place my hands around her rib cage. My thumbs are just under her breasts and my fingers meet on her spine. She makes me feel very protective and bit possessive...she is mine and I want to be hers. Her lips collide with mine and an explosion of heat consumes us. I try to restrain my demanding kiss to something more soft, more sensual, more loving...like her.

And in quick movement I change our positions. I place her on the bed resting, with my body tense and hovering hers. I breathe her in, her love, her beauty, her smell...her. I feel her small hands on my body exploring my back, my ribs, and my hair.

Her precious touch consumes me, and I insist on showing my passion for her with my mouth. My lips travel down her neck, across her chest and I reveal her breast. Beautiful, oh god she's beautiful. Her body responds to my every touch, and she makes soft subtle sounds in the back of her throat. I feel the vibrations with my lips, as I travel down her body to pay homage to her breast. I love this woman.

"Yes," escapes her mouths.

I kiss her breast and trace my tongue around her pebbled nipple. I gather the hem of her shirt in my hand and help move it over her head. My body moves up her body and we are breast to chest, and heat radiates from her.

My mouth continues to explore her chest up to her neck and take her mouth with mine. My hands begin to travel down her back to her shorts, and my fingers slip below the waistband. I feel my hips dig into her. My body is screaming for her.

...Stop, I don't want this. For the first time ever, I'm going to do this right.

I tear out of the room to find Emily at the door of her bedroom, head against the door crying. No sobbing. She stiffens as I touch her shoulder. "Are you in pain?" I ask hoping that that is the problem.

She doesn't turn around, so I gently touch her back with my hand. She spins around and glares at me with tears in her eyes and her forehead drawn in an extremely angry scowl.

"Emily, what's wrong?" I reach out for her and she pulls away.

"DON'T TOUCH ME!" I jump back at her words, but mostly at her anger. Her face contorts as her jaw clenches and her lips thin. I did this to her. My brain travels back, what happened? Did I push her too fast? Is she thinking of her late husband?

I soften my tone even more, "Talk to me. Tell me what I did?" I reach for her and she jerks away from me again and just shakes her head. Her eyes never leave mine as I watch her anger burn.

I don't walk away or move...I wait...I wait for her to calm down so I can find out what's wrong.

As she stares at me shooting daggers with her eyes, and I see unshed tears. After a long while her face changes from fury to...hurt?

I can't stand the hurt look in her eyes, and I pull her toward me to comfort her. She stiffens but doesn't pull away.

I rub my hands down her back to help sooth her, and feel her body become more rigid and she tries to take a step back. I don't relinquish my hold on her.

"I'm sorry. I'm sorry," was all I could think to say. I'm not sure what I did, but I'm sorry. I'm sorry she's hurt, I'm sorry she ran away from me, I'm sorry she's crying.

"I'm going to bed now," were the words that came from her mouth. The words were angry and bitter. Nothing like the precious woman I know.

"What happened?" I ask her, hoping she will give me a clue. Instead, she stiffens more and I can feel her body begin to shake. I relax my arm and she quickly turns away from me and grabs hold of the doorknob. She's about to bolt, again.

She is not running away, again. Oh, hell no! I put my arms around her pulling her back into my chest nuzzling my face in her neck...and I hold her...hold her as her body stiffens....hold her when her body begins to relax...hold her when she begins to cry...hold her when she stops...hold her until we both fall to the floor.

And then, I pull her into my lap, never breaking contact. Not giving her a chance to distance herself from me.

"Please, don't shut me out." I say burying my face in her back.

"I'm just giving you what you wanted." I here her soft, shaky voice say. What? I'm silent waiting for her to explain. She doesn't.

"What is it that you think I want?"

"I don't know, but you don't want this." She raises her head and looks at her door.

"The hell I don't. I want ALL of this." I want to laugh but I don't. I want her all of her, even the mad her, because she would be with me.

"You SAID you didn't want this." Oh my god, I said that out loud?

"I'm sorry. Oh my god, I'm so sorry." My hand snakes up onto her shoulder, as I pull myself even closer to her.

"I understand." My eyes widen at her statement.

"What exactly do you understand?"

"That you don't really feel like that about me. That we make better..." I spin her around so I see her face, and cut her off from saying something ridicules.

My lips crash into hers, and I pull her top lip with my teeth and my tongue demands entrance into her mouth. I deepen the kiss exploring her, worshipping her.

Growling I move her leg to straddle me, and I drag her waist pressing her petite frame against me. Our hips move together and she can feel the affect she has on my body. Slow, gentle kisses from before have no home in this passionate embrace. Her hand holds my shoulder in one and my nape in her other, and there is no room between us.

My hands immediately move under her shirt and lift it only up to her breast, but not exposing her. Our kisses become feral and my hands determine to say what my mouth cannot, yet. My hands urgently explore her back, her neck, her hair consantly pulling her closer to me, as our mouths consume each other. Our breaths are uneven and labored as I pull back to rest my forehead to hers, trying to regain the power of speech.

After some time, "You think I don't want you?" She doesn't say a word; she merely turns her head to look away. "Let me tell you what I want." I run my fingers over her cheek. "YOU."

"What I said...I didn't know I said it out loud. I was saying it to my self to remind me to calm down, to slow down, and do this right." I nuzzle her neck, breathing her in. "My body burns for you, I want you, but not just your body."

Her hand gives mine small squeezes, and she lowers her head. "Truth is, I would like to be buried so deep in you and not come out for a week...but I want so much more than that."

I tilt her chin to look at me, and caress her jaw with my thumb. "I'm almost 38 years old, too old to keep making the same mistakes. I don't want any mistakes with you." I rub my hand down the center of her chest. My fingers on her clavicle, my thumb rubbing circles over her heart. "I want to be buried in here first."

Her eyes are filled with tears again, but this time I see joy behind her them. I give her a weak smile, and press my lips to hers. I love you is what I feel and think, but it's too early to say.

"I am here, you know my intentions, and I will wait." My lips meet hers again.

She sinks into me. Her arms around my neck, her hands in my hair, and her body relaxes. I let out a deep breath and melt into her touch.

"Let me get you back in bed." She doesn't answer, but nods her head in agreement.

I move so I can pick her up from the floor, and I carry her to her bed. Gently laying her on a pillow, I move a lightweight blanket over her. Sitting beside her, I take her cheek in her hand. There are no words to say. This is about feeling and touching.

My fingers trace her face across her forehead, down the bridge of her nose, around her cheek, up her chin, and following the outline of her lips. Her eyes watch my face as my eyes are mesmerized by my fingers' actions.

"I'm sorry," she whispers in a weak voice.

"There is nothing to be sorry about." I lean over a kiss the tip of her nose.

"I over reacted."

"I don't know about that. In the heat of the moment hearing the words I said, I don't think it was an over reaction. But hopefully, I learned my lesson...don't think out loud."

She smiles at me and cups my cheek. I lean over and kiss her soft on the forehead; "I'll see you in the morning."

"Please don't go."

"I'll stay until you fall asleep."

"No, lay down with me. Hold me please." I relent, and lie down beside her.

I pull her into my body and wrap her with my arms, as the feeling of peace returns. Her fingers run up and down my chest, and I feel her fingers explore each muscle.

"I like your sounds." Her fingers are toying with my chest. "It's not a moan or a growl...it's more like a hum. You sound, I don't know, happy...relaxed. Does that sound dumb?"

"No, because that is exactly what I am. You have the power to calm me... well most of the time." I chuckle. She pulls her head back and looks at me.

"Earlier, when you were angry...not relaxing." I smile "And definitely your heated kisses are not relaxing."

I feel her smile, and I lean over and kiss her softly. Cherishing her.

Chapter 24 - You've Got a Week

There is nothing like staying at home for real comfort. - Jane Austen- Chapter 24 - You've got a WeekEmily's POV:My head feels heavy, and I don't quite have the energy to fully open my eyes, yet. Through my slits it is still dark and I can hear Cooper sleeping beside me. I smile.Bl inking my eyes open trying to focus to look at Cooper, his face is turned away from me. His breathing is slow and deep, he sounds peaceful. Moving closer I slide one hand under his pillow and wrap my other around his body to his heart. My body spoons his and I lay my cheek in the middle of his back. Giving in to fatigue listening to his heartbeat and his breathing, I fall asleep again.One of Cooper's hands runs up and down my arm, and the other rests on my thigh. "Hmmmm, this is a nice way to wake up," I hear him say in a husky, sleepy voice."Hmmm," is all I have the energy to say. After some time I ask, "What time is it?"He pulls away enough to see the clock...10:47."Are you kidding? I never sleep late."He chuckles, "You never sleep.""Yes, I do. It's gotten a lot better thank you."He turns around to face me. His fingers go straight to my hair. "How do you feel today?""Head fine, heart better." He smiles and it takes my breath away. I change the subject before any serious talk begins. "Don't you have to go to work today?""Are you trying to get rid of me?""Not at all," I say completely serious."I'm the boss. So, no, I don't have to go to work. The store manager can take care of any problems, and they can reach me if they need to." A mischievous smile creeps on his face. "What are your plans for today?""Well, since I don't have the kids, the only things on the list are choosing paint and checking on the garden.""Can we do that together?" His eyebrows rise toward his forehead."I would like that." He kisses my nose, "But first breakfast."He laughs and says, "It's almost lunch."He rolls out of bed. "Do you want some tea?""Yes, please."I walk into the kitchen and a shirtless Cooper is making coffee and heating water for tea. I watch as his the muscles in his back move. My eyes travel down south of his waistband...nice. It is a glorious site. This feels nice, and I smile because I am happy."Hey beautiful, are you checking me out." I know my face turns a bright shade of pink."Yes, is that a problem?""Not for me." He smiles so big and his face looks so youthful. He walks over toward me and kisses me on my lips, "Good morning." I could get used to this. It feels so nice, so...normal."You never told me. What time do the kids come back?" I ask."Not until tomorrow." His face lights up and I don't have to wonder long on what he is thinking. He bursts, "Change of plans. First date is tonight." He waggles his eyes at me, and I can't help but laugh. He's so adorable."Ok, time and place?""Now-all day including errands, and then maybe dinner or movie.""Either...both. I'm game." He picks me up and twirls me around. "Why are you so excited?""Because we can definitely say we are dating." He's quite funny right now. He adjusts his imaginary shirt and tie, "Seriously, I want to spend the day with you. Thank you." With that he kisses me softly, slowly taking in my lips and caressing my tongue with his. I don't think I'm going to get tired of this. -----"First stop, your store." I tell him as he open the passenger door of his BMW-SUV for me. This is the first time I've ridden in his vehicle. It's very nice and extremely clean. I can't even see a speck of dirt."What exactly are we getting at my store?" He asks as he kisses my nose and gets in the driver's seat."For the most part, paint. Michael is sending the painters tomorrow." He looks at me quizzically, "Basement and Mason's room." Still no hint of recognition. I let out an exasperated breath, knowing I've already had this conversation. "The basement is being finished and Mason is moving down there. The girls, including Addy, asked if I could make a girl guestroom for them.""Girl guestroom? I can't believe you said yes to that.""Well sort of, it's a kids bunk room. They chose purple, gray, and black as the colors and they will have two twin beds. They can girl it up from there." I watch his face as I talk. "When boys need it, I switch out for red blankets instead of purple. Everyone is happy, even me." He laughs as repeats 'girl it up.' As we get out in front of the store, I try to head in without him. He comes over to me, and laces his fingers in mine. My first thought is 'what will his employees think?' As if he's reading my mind, "Everyone will be happy. Don't worry." I wasn't worried for me.Mr. Frank, the older man at he counter, looks at us as we walk in, and smiles at us. "Hey boss, it looks like you caught you a good one.""You could say that again." Cooper squeezes my hand and smiles at me. I feel myself blush. I'm just hoping it's not too bright.Cooper leaves me to choose paint, while he checks something in his office. As the paint is mixed I choose a few brushes and some tape for another project. All the items are gathered, but he hasn't come back, yet.I walk back to where I think his office is, asking directions when I get out of the main storeroom. "Hey Mr. Mills, that woman that comes in here sometimes. The one you're always checking out. Well, I just saw her on the screen." I heard someone say. My heart sank a little.I hear Cooper as he moved through the room, "Well, where is she?""I don't know. I don't see her now, but boy, is she a looker.""Keep your eyes on your job." "Yes, sir."I take a deep breath and open the door."Boss, I found her again." My heart jumps in to my throat."Yes, I think you did." Cooper says not taking his eyes off of me. I turn to look at his employee at the monitors, and he is smiling with a huge grin."I'm finished. Are you almost ready to go?""Yes, I am." He introduces me to the staff, and he laces his fingers in mine as we leave the room."Were you watching someone in the store?" I ask hoping he wasn't."Yes," he says not hiding the fact from me. "You." I smile and let out a breath.This is the best and worst part of a new relationship. The best part because everything is new, and you're just getting to know each other. The worst part because you don't know each other enough to feel secure in the relationship.I know that when I'm with Cooper I feel secure, but he has a whole other world without me. It will take time.We stop for lunch at a great Mexican restaurant that serves fresh made tortillas and the most perfect salsa. A few people come to our table to say hi to Cooper, and he introduces me as his date. I swear each time he does I blush, and then he chuckles."On Saturday, we're going somewhere no one knows us." He smiles, "I don't think I will want to share."At Foster's house he helps me gather zucchini, yellow squash, and peppers. He helps me weed and water the garden, and then he takes me back home.Helping me wash the vegetables, Cooper asks, "Do you know what the best part of spending time with you now is?" I shake my head as he dries his hands, "Well, all of it, but now after a while I get to do this." He kisses me on the lips, taking my neck and running his hand up into my hair."We need to loose this." He pulls out the clip that was holding my hair, and my locks tumble past my shoulders. "Mmmm, better." His hands return to my hair running through each strand.I pull back, "We need to get the paint and supplies out of your vehicle. Then, we can do some more of this." "Promise.""Yes, and I keep my word." He follows me out to his SUV and he carries the paint as I bring the bags."Are you going to give me a grand tour?" He asks deposit all of the items in my basement.I give him a tour of my construction zone. "Why have you waited so long to finish this?""My needs have changed since the plan was first drawn. I had to work with Michael to come up with a new layout. We have two bedrooms, a bath, a game room, and a safe room.""From the outside, no one would ever know your house was this big.""I know, that's how I like it, but it's still a bit small for the neighborhood. Even with this area completed.""Most people around here are more about show than substance, but not you. You are very different, in the best possible way." He leans in and gives me a sweet kiss on the forehead. "I didn't even look. What colors did you pick?""Dove gray for the bedrooms, including Mason's old room, and soft, sage green for the rest of the area...with white trim throughout.""Sounds nice."We walk to the backyard from the basement, and climb up to the deck. The sun was just going down behind the trees, and the only sound was from the wind."It's peaceful back here," he says he sits beside me."I know. I'm becoming spoiled." He laces his fingers in mine and rubs his thumb over my knuckles."I'm planning on keeping you that way." He lifts my hand to his lips.Cooper's POV:She said I had a week, and I have made the most of it. On Sunday afternoon, she leaves for Boston for a week. Then to Nashville for another week while Mason is at soccer camp at some college.We spent the whole day and most of the night together Monday. Tuesday the kids came back and we were invited to Will's house to play in the pool. We sat the kids down (Mason and Addy) and let them know that we were dating. Both of them took it well. Addy was ecstatic and Mason just nodded, but in the 'You better be good to my mom' kind of way.Pizza and movie night was Wednesday, but I sat with Emily on the deck just holding hands.Thursday Linda, Garrett and the kids returned home from a vacation. They came over for a few hours. Friday was chaotic. I left work at lunch to help Emily and Mason as they were preparing to be gone for two weeks. Washing clothes, packing, cleaning out the fridge...chaos. Peyton was happy just playing with Addy and me as Emily did her thing. By 6:00 we all left to visit her parents. We thought it would be easier if we were able to leave Addy and the boys with her parents, while we spent time together on Saturday.Here I am bright and early on Saturday morning, knocking on her parents' door. She has no idea what we are doing today, but I did let her know she would need a change of clothes...at least one.She greets me at the door. Her hair is braided laying over one shoulder, and she looks like a dream. I touch her face, and rub my thumb across her cheek. "Good morning.""Good morning to you, too."Jim clears his throat, and he has my full attention. "This is my baby, and only daughter. Keep her safe, and treat her like the lady she is." His warning was stern, but enduring."Yes, sir. With my life.""What time will you be back?" I walk over to him and explain my plans in a hushed voice so Emily doesn't hear. "Ok, have fun.""Ok, Mr. Planner, where to first?"

She asks as we turn off her parents' road."Home.""Are you serious? I spent the night at my parents' house just so we can drive an hour and half back home?" She's laughing at me. "Lead on." She is very trusting."You missed the turn." I don't say anything to her. Just smile. "Is there a short cut I don't know about?"I keep driving. "You're taking me to the river." She sounds so cute and happy. "I love the river.""I didn't know that." There are still a lot of things I don't know about this lady."It's one of my favorite place. Do you fish?""Yes, fly...no bait. How about you?""I fly fish, but I don't have a license." One day soon, I need to get her out in the water.She watches the scenery, trying to figure out where exactly we were going. I sort of like her left in the dark. She is a little antsy and damn cute."Where are we?" She asks as I turn into a driveway."Home." Her quizzical look makes me laugh. "This is my home." With the looks she gives me, I have some explaining to do. "My house is Shadow Creek belonged to my sister. I kept it so Addy wouldn't have too many changes too fast. But this is my home." Her face lit up when she took in the craftsman style house before her."I already love it. Did you have this built?""Yes. I saw the plans one day, and I tweaked the design a little to suit my needs.""I can't wait to see the inside." She walks slowly taking in the charm of the cedar shake and stone façade. I open the door, and I hear her take a breath."It's amazing. It's so beautiful." I watch her walk around my house, and picture her being here all the time. I give her a grand tour, and I can tell from her face that she truly loves this place. I save the best for last."Through here." She walks out on the deck, from the living room the view is nice, but..."Oh," I hear her breath catch. "This is breathtaking." Stepping out on the deck, one has a better view of the river. The early morning fog hasn't burned off, yet, and you can see the fly fisherman out in the water. "You gave this up for Addy?""No, I gave up living here full time for Addy." She smiles at me and kisses me for the first time today. Right now, in this spot, with this lady, I am in heaven. We eat breakfast on the deck, and spend the next several hours exploring my house and walking to down to the river bank. Every so often I would stop and worship her with kisses. We did a lot of silly first date things like:

favorite color- hers green, mine maroon; birthdays- hers September 8, mine July 1; favorite all time movie- hers To Kill a Mockingbird, mine- Rear Window; wish you could visit- hers Florence, mine coast of South Africa. I have lunch delivered, because I was true to my word. I did not want to share her today. Considering she will leave tomorrow for two weeks, I am definitely keeping her to myself.Just before dusk, we climb back into my vehicle. "I hope you're ready for this." She's changed into a long flowing white skirt and a sleeveless green top, and she looks precious."If it's as sweet as your first surprise, I think I am.""It's probably not, but it is fun."Our drive is long, but the music and conversation is wonderful. By the time we reach the little town of Marshall it is dark, and we turn into one of the last drive in theaters in the state."Oh, this is fun." She smiles, and her face lights up.We park, tune the radio to the right station, pop the back of the SUV, and lay out a blanket and a few pillows. She wiggles herself into a comfortable place and laughs at me, while I try to use electrical tape over the interior lights. She leans into my chest and for the next few hours we are together...no one else. I don't even know what movie we watched.__________Please vote and/or comment...your feedback is great encouragement. Thank you.Posted a picture of Cooper's House

Chapter 25 - Time to Come Home

A bsence is to love what wind is to fire; it extinguishes the small, and enkindles the great. - Roger de Rabutin

Chapter 25 - Time to Come Home

Emily's POV:

Whoever said absence makes the heart grow fonder is an idiot. Absence makes the heart lonely.

My week in Boston so far has been bliss, except I miss Cooper. I had been planning on this visit since I was invited at Christmas, and now part of me wishes that I had not come...the part that misses Cooper, that is.

My friends Saada and Niam have kept the boys and me busy. We went to the Cape, visited museums, walked the Freedom Trail, attended a concert in the park, and visited every college in the area. Saada accepted a fellowship at Harvard a year and a half ago and was excited to show us, mostly Mason, around. Her hope is for him to choose a New England university, so he would be close to her, and I would have to come out and visit more. Actually, those were her words.

I met Naim shortly after we moved to North Carolina; he was Mason's pediatrician. About two hours after his first appointment, I ran to the store to pick a few small items, and Dr. Hasni was there. "Hey, mom isn't that my doctor?" Mason had asked in a 'not even close' to an inside voice. Niam got a good laugh out of my child's excitement, and we exchanged pleasantries. We talked again two weeks later when Dr. Hasni was out mowing the yard at a house beside Mason's new best friend. He had just moved in that weekend. A few months later Mason had gotten strep throat, and Dr. Hasni remembered us. He had just gotten married and was anxious for his wife to find new friends. He thought that I was a sweet lady (his words) and that I would be kind to his new wife. His marriage had been arranged, at the time he was 37 and Saada was 25 and fresh out of medical school. He wanted his bride to feel comfortable. Saada and I became instant friends, and that was nearly seven years ago.

Patrick had liked the Hasnis. As a couple we had a few things in common, one of which was age difference. Patrick and I were eight years apart, and the Hasnis were twelve. This difference never bothered me, and by the way Saada and Niam are together, it doesn't bother them either.

Cooper and I have talked each night, and have even texted a few times a day...each day. Saada teased me about being a teenager, again. She thought it was cute.

Cooper and I set up a time to SKYPE. Right now Mason had taken over the computer, so he could talk to Addy. I'm a bit anxious for my turn, and I walk in the room to move the conversation along.

"Is he still bothering you?" Mason asks.

"No, now he just ignores me when I'm at his house."

"Good, I gave him that as an option. It is better than him harassing you." I keep listening. I don't like the idea that someone is harassing my little Addyson.

"It is better, but I wish he could just be nice like he was before."

"I'll be home in a few days, and you can hang out with me if you want to."

"Good, that would be great." I'll talk with Mason about this conversation later. He's concerned about Addy, and so am I.

Peyton came in with Saada and Naim, and Peyton takes over the conversation with Addy. I can see Cooper behind her now, impatiently waiting to talk to me. "He's quite a looker," Saada whispers.

"Yes, I know. I find myself staring at him a lot. He is completely distracting."

"I can see that." Niam clears his throat loudly, and Saada blushes and apologizes, sort of.

"Coop, can you see me. You're in my c'puter." Peyton says as he tilts his head to the side like he's trying to see around Addy.

"Hello Peyton. Are you being a good boy?"

"Yes, but I didn't take a nap today. I was pwaying too big." I like how he says playing.

"How is your mom? Is she being good?"

"Yes, she takes me pwaying. We went to the shower rocks today."

"Shower rocks?" Cooper's face twist up like he is confused, so does Addy's.

I speak over Peyton, "It's a fountain at Harvard. Water mists out between the rocks."

Cooper turns his head toward the direction I was standing, but I was off screen. "Thanks." He turns his attention back to Peyton. "Did you get to touch the water?"

"Yep, and then I had to change cwothes. You want go see it?" Any 'L' blend word still gives him a bit of trouble some articulation, but his command of language is pretty good.

"I would like to, but maybe some other time."

His conversation continued for a few more minutes, before Niam asks to talk to Cooper alone. Saada ushers me out of the room, and we get Peyton ready for bed. "He seems like a nice man. He is good with your sons?"

"He is nice, and he's good with both of my boys."

"His eyes sparkle when he talks to you." He didn't talk to me. "When he heard your voice, his eyes lit up. You are a lucky woman. To have the love of two such men."

I know my look shows the confusion I feel. "What?"

"Patrick was a good man, and he loved you very much. This man, talking to Niam...he loves you, too." Cooper loves me?

Naim opens the door and lets me know Cooper would like to talk to me.

I sat down at the computer, and Cooper gives me a smile. His eyes sparkle a little as he takes a moment to look at me. This is the same way he has looked at me for months, the look I never understood. This is the one I used to think was strange, because he only looks this way when he looks at me. This is the look that makes me catch my breath.

"It's good to see you. I've missed you." I do not hesitate to tell him.

His face becomes more serious. "I've missed you, too." I drink in his words, watching him, memorizing him. It will be more than a week, before I get to see him in person.

"What are you and Addy up to tonight?"

"We were going to go bowling with Will and Chandler, but I think that's been nixed for the pool, instead." He half rolls his eyes, as I know he's talking about the girls constantly changing their minds. He is quite adorable. "What about you? Big plans for the evening?"

"No, our evening is almost finished. I helped Saada cook, and we are staying in. Tomorrow Niam is taking us to a New England Revolution game. Mason is excited even if he doesn't follow either of the teams."

"New England Revolution?"

"Soccer...what else?" He laughs because he should know that my boy lives and breathes soccer. "I was hoping to catch a Red Sox game, but Mason told me that watching paint dry would be more fun than that."

Cooper laughs more, and he has a boyish look to his face. "He's probably right, if he only watches baseball on television. It's much different to watch a game live."

"That's what I tried to tell him, but I'm only the mother."

"We should go see the Cardinals play sometime. He would like a live game." He offers.

"I would love that." The look on Cooper's face is priceless. It's something between happy and shock.

"Hold on, let me get this right. You are agreeing to go to a sporting event with me?"

"Yes."

"I thought..."

"You have proven yourself able to do something other than sports together." I smile at him. "For the record I like sports, but I also like other things."

"Duly noted." His face is more serious now. "When will you be home?"

"A week from Saturday, but it will be very late. Mason's camp plays a scrimmage game, and then he meets the coach for an evaluation, and then we will drive home."

He has a curious look. "I thought you were flying?"

"No, we flew to Boston and will fly to Nashville, but I'm driving home. It's only a few hour drive." I give him a small smile, trying to erase the concerned look off of Cooper's face.

We talk some more, and then say goodnight. It's a little bit hard on me to be away from Cooper.

Cooper's POV:

"Up and at 'em, little bit." Addy is struggling to wake up. Usually, she's easy to wake up in the morning, but she must not have gotten much sleep last night. She twists her face up at me, and she looks just like her mother. "Get dressed and I'll let you sleep in the vehicle."

We are on the road within 20 minutes. Addy talks to me for a little while before she fades off to sleep. Six long hours later, Addy and I are at the outskirts of Nashville.

Me: Where are you?

Emily: Zoo, with Peyton

Me: He have fun?

Emily: lots…we're on our way to watch Mason's scrimmage

Me: Have fun. Miss you

Emily: Miss you, too

I google Lipscomb University, send the address to my GPS, and head out to find Emily. Addy is taking in the sites of Nashville, wondering if Emily and Peyton will be happy to see us. I wonder the same thing.

Mason is easy to spot on the field. He's running drills, warming up to play keeper. He looks more confident than he did during the season. There are very few spectators in the stands, making it easy to find Emily. She's sitting quietly holding a sleeping Peyton to her chest. They both look exhausted. Her eyes are closed as she rests her cheek on Peyton's forehead. She has such a gentle, tender look on her face.

Her eyes flicker open and they lock on mine. Without a word between us, I know this was the right decision to surprise her in Nashville. Her face first registers as shock, and then the smile. The smile that she seems to only give to me grew across her face, and I couldn't wait to kiss her.

While I was busy taking in the site of her, Addy had bounces up the bleachers and was moving down to her ahead of me. "Oh, Addy, I've missed you." She gives her a sideways hug, trying not to wake up Peyton.

"I've missed you, too. How long until Peyton wakes back up." Addy asks wanting to play little momma to him, I'm sure.

"He fell asleep in the car. He'll probably be out for another hour, unless he gets too hot." For June in the south, this is a very comfortable weather, and I doubt Peyton will wake up early.

"Hi beautiful." I press my lips to hers and whisper, "I have a lot more of those to give you later."

Her face beams as she looks at me, and I know my expression mirrors hers. It's been twelve very long days without her. That is just too long.

"Hi, I can't believe you're here."

"I couldn't wait any longer for you to come home. Remember, I'm not really a patient man." She laughs at my truthful comments. I take a spot beside her, running my fingers down her arm to her hand.

"But you're patient with me."

"Yes, but I'd do anything for you."

"Good to know." A mischievous expression plays on her face. "I'll first take another kiss. Then, I'll start making a list."

Leaning over, I kiss her lips again...soft and a little less chaste, but I am reserving the rest of later. "You just do that."

After the scrimmage Mason runs over to meet his mom. I take a still sleeping Peyton from her arms, as she readjusts her shirt, and tries to smooth the wrinkles as she walks to talk with Mason. She asks how he thought he was doing, giving him time to tell her where he felt confident. Then, she tells him what she sees as an improvement. She would not let him tell her about any of his failures.

"You have time with the coach to beat yourself up. I'm here for your encouragement. You can tell me what your coach says, after you meet with him." Her voice is soft and firm. He nods his head into submission. This must be an ongoing thing with them.

"Cooper, Addy, I didn't know you guys were coming." Mason says but his eyes never left Addy.

"We didn't know until yesterday." I place my hand on Addy's back. "She's been missing you guys almost as much as I have."

"You have?" The question was directed to Addy, and she nods her answer. A whistle blows. "I've got to go. Will I see you tomorrow?"

"Yes. Same time." Emily tells him as she laces her fingers in mine.

"Bye, Mason." Addy high fives him before he heads back across the field.

"Ok, so what are plans now?" I ask.

"I don't have any. I usually head back to the hotel to play in the pool after I see Mason."

Addy squeals, "I want to go swimming." My finger goes to my mouth to gesture for to be quieter, and she slaps her hand over her mouth and murmurs, "Sorry."

"Ok, swimming it is." We walk out to the parking. "Where did you park?"

I pulled out the keys and push the button on the remote with my eyes steady on hers. "You brought the suburban?"

"You shouldn't let Michael have an extra key, he will let anyone drive it." She smiles brightly at me. "I thought you may need a lift home, after we ditch your rental."

"Thank you." She drives her car over to me, and we move Peyton's car seat. We adjust him in the back seat with Addy by his side, and I follow her to return the car. Then, check into Embassy Suites.

"My belly hurts, momma." Peyton says as he exits the pool. Emily picks him up, brushes the hair away from his eyes, and kisses him.

"Maybe it's time to change clothes and maybe go get some dinner." She looks over at me and I nod in agreement. It's time for dinner.

Addy walks Peyton to the elevator and picks him up for him to push the button. "Look I'm big."

"Yes you are." I say as he smiles at everyone around. He has a way of gathering everyone's attention by even the littlest things.

After dinner, Peyton and Emily sprawl across Emily's bed to watch Happy Feet. "Are the kids settled?" I ask, patting a space beside me on the couch.

She walks over to me, leans down, and kisses me. "Yes, do you want anything while I'm up?" I shake my head no as she reaches in the fridge for a bottle of water. "I still can't get over you being here."

"I came for purely selfish reasons."

"Oh, yeah. What are those?" Emily smiles at me as I touch the side of her face. My thumb rubs across her cheekbone, and I urge her to meet my lips. Our lips touch chastely at first, but before I could deepen the kiss, she ran her tongue over my top lip, making me smile at her forwardness. I gave her a moment to explore my jaw and ear before I meet her lips again. This time my tongue softly delves into her mouth, and I hear her sigh. "I've missed you. I've missed this."

I chuckle, and continue kissing this incredibly sexy, precious woman. She kisses like a dream, or at least like every dream I've had lately. I have missed her so much. My hand moves from her face to her neck and hair, and all the while my lips continue to shower her will affection.

"We've got to stop, or at least slow down. The kids are in the next room ...and the door is wide open." She is the epitome of calm, cool, collected lady to the outside world. In private she has shown me lust and anger, but I know that we are not in private. Her words remind me that we may get an unwanted audience. I readjust my sitting; so she can easily lean into me, and I can still kiss her face.

"What is on the agenda for tomorrow?"

"I haven't made plans, yet. I've been coming up with plans in the morning, after I check the weather and Peyton's mood."

I laugh, "Have you been dealing with a moody two year old?" She rolls her eyes at me. "You have no idea."

Our morning was made up with a trip to Belmont Plantation and lunch on the riverfront. By 3:00 we were back at Lipscomb to see the last scrimmage of the day. Addy was holding Emily's hand and they are wearing bright colored sundresses. Addy's was pink of course, and Emily's was sort of a mint green. Peyton was wanting me to carry him, and we are walking a few feet behind our lovely ladies.

There is a small commotion across from us in the parking lot, but it is easy to ignore. I can hear Emily gasp, "I'm so sorry. I didn't know..." She turns toward me with almost a panicked look.

She isn't able to say anything else before, "He's barely cold in the ground and you're already playing house with someone else." A woman not much older than Emily spat, "I would love to say this shocks me, but it doesn't." I've never heard anyone talk to Emily in anger...I don't like it.

I move to Emily's side, moving ahead of her, closer to the woman, trying to take gain the woman's focus. "Do not speak to her like that."

"What's wrong Emily, you can't talk for yourself?" Emily stands there silently with her chin up and her shoulder's squared.

"Excuse me, do not speak to her. Who do you think you are?" Emily faces me, and gives me a small smile.

"I'm sorry. Cooper this is Regan Cahill Bartelt, Regan this is Cooper Mills." Emily says with such poise, that I almost forget I want to hit this venomous bitch. Emily puts her hand in mine, squeezes it and looks at me, "This is Patrick's sister." I'm not sure how, but Emily is able to ease tension with just a touch.

She turns back to Regan and asks, "Are your parents here, also?" Emily's face is soft and pleasant when she is talking. If it weren't for the tenseness in her body, one would never know she was uncomfortable.

"You know they're not. They are always in the Keys this time of year. That's probably why you chose now to come for a visit." A vein pulses in this woman's forehead. "That's why they sent me, making sure you're taking care of my nephew. Where is he anyway?" I turn my body so Peyton is farther way from this woman.

"He's out on the field. Would you like to watch him play?"

"Yes, but not with you." She snarls and walks off.

"I'm so sorry. I didn't know she was coming. I would have warned you."

"She's not a nice person." Addy interjects. That is an understatement.

"I don't like her, and I don't like how she talks to you. Why do you stand there and take it?" I feel myself getting angry first at that woman, and then at Emily for allowing it.

"What exactly would it have accomplished if I lost my temper, and show her that her words hurt?" I shake my head.

"I don't know, but it looks like you just gave her permission to do it again." I'm talking through clenched teeth to keep from yelling.

"She's not going to change her opinion of me. This isn't new. She treated me like this before I married Patrick. This is how it has always been. I've just been lucky I rarely see her."

"Didn't Patrick stop her?"

"Yes, but it did no good. As soon as he was out of the room she would begin, again. I have been mad, screamed, and yelled at her...she laughed. Patrick made sure we had limited contact with her, and fortunately I have only seen her a few times since Mason was born."

'So, now you choose not to deal with her. You just let her run all over you." She shakes her head in disbelief.

"I'm not letting her run all over me. I'm choosing to ignore her anger." Emily walks away in the exact manner that she was walking before...without a care in the world.

"Make me understand this." I tell her as we sit to watch Mason. "Tell me how you stay calm, when all I want to do is punch her lights out?"

"Don't look at me like that, Cooper. I'm not a saint. I'm waiting for the day she physically touches me. Me being calm makes her mad...livid, in fact. CJ and Michael taught me how to defend myself. Patrick made sure my skills stayed sharp. She touches me, I will take her out." She whispers, "And I will win."

Pride is the only word that can describe how I feel at this very second. My sweet, angelic lady is a scrapper.

"I still don't like how she talks to you. You are far too important to me to be disrespected."

"Thank you, but this is one battle I will fight on my own." She squeezes my hand.

"You can't tell me her words didn't hurt."

"No, they hurt, but the are also untrue. This..." She gestures between us. "may be early in some people's eyes, but we both know that it took a while to get here. We're not playing house, nor did I replace Patrick with you. As long as the two of us are ok, who cares what she says?"

God, I love this woman...